KISS
by
MOONLIGHT

SUNWALKER SAGA - BOOK FOUR

SHÉA MACLEOD

Sunwalker
Press

Kissed by Moonlight
Sunwalker Saga, Book 4
Text copyright © 2013 Shéa MacLeod
All rights reserved.
Printed in the United States of America.

Dedication

For Lili who enjoys a Grand Adventure.

Acknowledgments

As with all the books in the Sunwalker universe, I try to describe real places as accurately as possible. Sometimes, however, I take a little bit of creative license. For instance, the Shanghai Tunnels are real and you can still tour them today (though there is some debate between historians as to whether or not they were actually used for shanghaiing). The tunnels are not, however, quite as I've described them as I've made them quite a bit more extensive than I believe they are today.

As always, thanks to all those who helped me create this story by brainstorming, beta reading, and generally kicking me in the backside. A giant THANK YOU to my beta readers, critique partners, and editors. This story wouldn't be half what it is without them. Thanks once again to my uncle, Jim, who answered my questions regarding Tribal land and legal procedures. Any errors there are mine.

Prologue

Previously...

I watched in horror as a huge hole opened up in Inigo's chest. Blood spilled down the front of his shirt, soaking his clothing in seconds. He crumpled to the ground.

"No!" I sank to my knees on the cold marble floor, reaching toward the water, but with another wave of the queen's hand, the image went dark. "No, no, no!" I screamed until my throat was raw, pawing at the water as though I could slip through it back to my own world.

"Why?" was all I could get out past the agonizing tightness of my throat. I could barely see the queen for the tears that welled in my eyes and spilled down my cheeks. All I could do was lie on the icy floor as agony burned its way through my chest.

The smile she gave me was so far from human, I could hardly comprehend it. "For the death of a Sidhe, there is always a price, Morgan Bailey."

Chapter 1

My legs had gone to sleep. That was the only thing that saved my life.

One moment I was kneeling on the bitterly cold black marble of the Other World staring at the dark pool of water, willing it to work again. To show me that copse of trees in the high desert where my friends waited. To show me Inigo.

The next, I was collapsing sideways as my legs gave out. Pins and needles shot through me from toes to mid-thigh. As I teetered to the left, a large axe buried itself in the floor beside me with a clang, metal biting into smooth stone. If I hadn't fallen over, it would have been buried in my skull.

"Holy sh…"

My legs mostly useless, I wriggled around the edge of the pool like a snake, the slick marble easing my way. Another clang of metal against stone. I turned to stare at the axe, which had missed my foot by an inch. What kind of metal could damage marble like that? For that matter, how the heck had someone gotten metal into the Other World? The Sidhe hated metal and prevented it from entering their kingdom. My knives never came through with me. The axe couldn't possibly be Earth metal.

I scrambled out of the way as the axe's wielder yanked the weapon free. My brain tried to make sense of what I was seeing, but it was having trouble catching up. The axe-man was huge, at least seven feet tall, and had muscles that would have made The Rock weep with envy. Thick legs were encased in leather pants, and silver-studded leather straps strained across his massive, tattooed chest. But the thing that really caught my attention was that he had the head of a boar.

Not like a cute little pink pig from a farm. A freaking boar with enormous, curved yellow tusks dripping with saliva. Head, neck, and shoulders were covered in grayish brown bristles. He glared at me with hateful red eyes and let out an angry squeal that had my stomach doing panicked flip flops. I had no doubt he intended to kill me.

"Morgana!" I shrieked, praying that, despite what she'd done, the fairy queen would hear me and send help. "Morgana!"

There was no answer. The giant boar man kept coming, swinging that wicked axe, and here I was without a single weapon and no access to my Atlantean powers. For whatever reason, they didn't work on the Other Side.

But you are still a hunter. Act like one.

Wrapping my fingers around the edge of the pool to anchor myself on the slippery marble, I lashed out with both feet, slamming them straight into the creature's right patella. He dropped to the floor with a crash and a pig-like scream, deadly axe skittering across the smooth surface.

I had to get that axe.

I staggered to my feet and charged awkwardly around the pool toward the weapon. My legs were finally working again. Sort of. I still had that funny pins-and-needles tingly feeling and I definitely felt off kilter, but adrenaline lent me speed if not agility.

Close up the axe was enormous. I wrapped one hand around the wooden shaft, which had to be at least double the length and diameter of a normal axe. My fingers barely went all the way around it. The head reminded me of those Viking war axes they always showed in the movies, except it was double-sided and a hell of a lot bigger.

I yanked hard, but the axe didn't move an inch. It was so heavy, I hadn't even managed to shift it. Definitely not Earth metal.

"Holy shit, what is this thing made of?"

Wrapping both hands around the shaft, I tried to lift. This time, I managed to get it off the floor by a whole inch. Even with my extra hunter strength, this baby was going nowhere, and the man boar thing was getting to his feet. I swear I could see puffs of steam coming out of his ears.

So I did the only thing that came to mind. I started dragging the axe across the floor toward the pool. If I couldn't arm myself, I could disarm my opponent. Maybe.

The axe head made a gods-awful shriek against the stone, scratching a deep furrow in the black marble. What the nine hells was this thing made out of? Some kind of Asgard metal? The man boar swiveled his head in my direction, his tiny red pig eyes glaring at me, massive shoulder muscles bunching. He let out a squeal that sent a chill down my spine.

Lowering his head, he charged straight at me so fast I barely had time to drop the axe and dance out of the way. The creature seemed surprised he'd missed as he stumbled to a halt and shook his head. He let out another one of those bone-chilling squeals; clearly, I'd frustrated him.

Not waiting for the next charge, I grabbed the axe again and gave another good heave. Closer this time. I had no idea how deep the pool was, but hopefully deep enough Pig Man couldn't get to it easily. One more heave, and it would be in the water.

Too late. The beast charged again, and this time he didn't make the mistake of giving me time to get out of the way. Instead, he tackled me, grabbed me around the waist and knocked me off my feet.

Fortunately for my spine, the tackle drove me backward before I went down. I braced myself for the marble, but instead I hit water.

I plunged into the fairy pool with Pig Man on top me. Holding my breath as the dark water closed over my head, I waited for the jolt of hitting the bottom, but I just kept sinking.

***

I was falling through cold black water, desperate for a breath of air, and then all I could see was endless blue sky. The icy winter air chilled me to my bones as I drew it in. Then I hit the frozen ground. The air rushed out of my lungs, leaving me struggling to draw my next breath.

With a gasp, I finally sucked air into my lungs. I needed to move before the boar man fell on me, but my arms and legs didn't want to work. I stared up at the cloudless sky and wondered vaguely why the Other World looked just like Earth. And also why I wasn't getting squished by a monster pig man.

Spots danced in my vision, and my skull felt a little tight. I was going to have a gods-awful headache. My clothes were still dry, which I found odd. Shouldn't I be sopping wet?

"Morgan." A face appeared above me, swimming in and out of focus. Short, sun-streaked hair. Ocean blue eyes.

"Jack?" It came out as barely more than a squeak. I hadn't quite gotten my breath back yet.

Another face popped into view. "Oh my goddess, Morgan. Are you okay?"

I squinted, trying to bring Kabita's features into focus. I could make out her warm cinnamon skin and curly black hair, but everything else was blurry still. "Uh, yeah, I think so. You didn't happen to see a man boar?"

Kabita and Jack exchanged glances as if to say 'She's off her rocker again.' The cold was seeping through my clothes, making me shiver, but sitting up was beyond me at the moment.

"Uh, no. Where the hell did you go?" Kabita demanded. "One minute you were here, and the next you vanished into thin air."

I ignored her. I only had one thing on my mind now that pig man was gone. I needed to know what the queen had done. "Inigo. Where's Inigo?"

Another glance passed between them. I could tell by their faces something was very wrong. Not that I needed them to tell me that. I'd seen it for myself, thanks to the fairy queen and that dark pool of water.

She'd flicked her finger, and a hole had opened up in Inigo's chest. I'd been helpless as the man I loved crumpled to the ground, lifeless. And then Morgana, the Queen of the Sidhe, had walked away as if it meant nothing.

"Help me up," I demanded, holding my hand out. Nobody took it. "I said, help me up."

"Morgan, you fell. You could be injured…"

"I didn't ask for your medical opinion, Jack," I snapped. "Help me up, or so help me gods, I will rip you limb from limb."

He helped me up. I doubt it was because he was afraid of me. Jack was about as immortal as they came and a hell of a lot stronger than I'd ever be. But now that I was back on Terra Firma, my abilities had kicked back in, which meant any damage I'd sustained during the fall had probably already healed.

The minute I was on my feet, I realized we were only about a hundred yards away from the copse of juniper trees that had been the final battle ground against the would be fairy king, Alberich. The same place I'd watched from the Other World as the fae queen took the life of the man I loved.

Kabita laid her hand on my arm. "There's something you should know."

"I already do." And with that, I took off, running across the uneven ground, dodging scraggly sage brush and crushing tumbleweeds under my boots. I darted between the trees and into the center of the copse, where I came to a dead stop.

The man standing there, waiting for me, was hauntingly beautiful. He smelled of chocolate and campfires, and his eyes glittered with gold and mysteries. The smile he gave me was so full of sadness, it broke my heart. What was left of it.

"Drago." It was the only thing I could get out past the tightness in my chest.

"I am so sorry, Morgan."

Then and only then did I break down and cry.

***

He lay crumpled on the ground, skin pale as death. Around him the grass, now dry and brown with winter cold, waved gently in the chilly breeze that rustled the juniper boughs. I wiped away hot tears as I ran to him.

"Oh, Ingo," I whispered, kneeling beside his still form. "I'm so sorry. I couldn't stop her." I brushed a stray lock of dark blond hair away from his forehead. Someone had removed his glasses, or maybe they'd fallen off when he'd... when the queen... Fuck dammit.

My throat felt like someone had taken a hot cigarette lighter from a car and jammed it down in there, a huge lump that choked and burned and made me want to throw up. The blood covering his chest was dry, not that I cared. I lay my head down next to the gaping wound as though I could still hear his heartbeat, but there was nothing. Only the sound of the wind and the gentle distant murmur from my friends.

Arms wrapped around me, too big to be Kabita, too gentle to be Jack. "I'm so sorry, Morgan." Trevor Daly's voice was soft in my ear. "It happened so fast. There was nothing we could do. We don't even know why..."

"It was her," I told my brother. "Morgana. It was the fairy queen's revenge for killing Alberich. She made me watch." I choked on the sob that rose in my throat.

"Oh my god." Trevor's arms tightened around me as I pressed my face against his leather jacket. The horror in his voice almost undid me. So much sorrow and anguish flooded my soul, I thought I might actually die of it.

I felt another hand on my shoulder, and I knew from the scent it was Drago. "It's time," he said, as if I should know what that meant. I pulled against his hand, refusing to leave Inigo. I would stay here with him until...

I squeezed my eyes shut. I hadn't seen his soul leave his body like I had Zip's. Of course, I could have missed it, being in the Other World. It was ridiculous, but I was afraid to leave in case he was still trapped in there somewhere.

"Come on, Morgan." This time it was Trevor who tried to pull me away from Inigo's body.

"What? No." I resisted his gentle tug. "I'm not going anywhere without Inigo."

"I'm sorry, but you must." Drago's voice held an edge of authority that rubbed me the wrong way. Yes, he was Inigo's half-brother and a king, but they had only met a few months ago. Inigo and I had been friends for years. More than that, he was my boyfriend. My rock.

Trevor pulled a little harder. I jerked away from him.

"Why is he here?" I snarled at my brother, glaring at Drago as though this were all his fault.

"I called him."

My eyes widened. "What?"

Drago knelt down to my level. His inhuman eyes stared straight into mine, as though he could will me to understand. "Listen to me, Morgan. If we are to save him, you must let me take him now. Before it's too late."

It was as if he was speaking Chinese or something. I could hear the words but they weren't making any sense.

"I don't understand." I lay my palm against Inigo's chest where his heartbeat should be. It was so still. "He's…" I couldn't say "dead." It might make it all real. "Gone."

Drago laid his hand next to mine. I noted vaguely that his tanned skin shimmered slightly in the weak winter sun, as if there were a little gold embedded in it. A wry smile twisted his full lips. "Not quite."

Hope, that cruel little devil, sprang up inside me. "What do you mean?"

He stood and offered me his hand. "We're dragons, remember. We are not that easy to kill."

Chapter 2

Icy water slid through trails of thick, green slime to pool at the base of the rock walls. Torchlight glittered off a billion tiny crystals embedded in the stone. The air was cold and wet. Not at all what I expected from a dragon cave.

Cordelia's sister Sandra—now calling herself Tanith—walked beside me in complete silence. She'd explained to me that once we entered the caves, we were not to utter a single word. The only reason the dragons were allowing us to visit one of their most sacred places was because Sandra - I mean Tanith - was their Dragon Child. The first in centuries. As for me, I was the Fire Bringer. I still had no idea what that meant, but it was important to the dragons and allowed me a certain leeway. Believe me, I was taking advantage.

Drago hadn't wanted me with him when he took Inigo's body back to dragon land, deep within the Scottish highlands, but I hadn't been about to take no for an answer. I think he might have been worried that, if he left me behind, I'd just get on a plane and follow. So, he'd given in and ordered one of his beefy bodyguards to take me on his back.

The first time I'd flown to dragon lands had been on Inigo's back. It had been exhilarating. In dragon form, Inigo wasn't much bigger than a horse, which made for a fairly comfortable ride, and his mind-speaking talents made for all sorts of fun. Drago's bodyguard was substantially bigger, which made staying on his back a challenge. Either he didn't have mind-speak, or he didn't deign to use it, which was fine by me. It was a long, miserable journey made worse by bone-deep sorrow and the gaping hole inside me created by Inigo's loss warring with the smidgeon of hope he could still be saved.

Tanith was the first person I saw once we'd landed. She hadn't said a word, just folded me in her arms and let me cry right there in front of the gods and everybody. Nobody'd seemed bothered by my show of grief, and a few even joined me in shedding tears.

Tanith had led me to a room within the dragons' main citadel, where we waited for Drago to finish performing the ritual that would put Inigo in stasis. That was one thing about which the Dragon King would not budge: no humans allowed. While we waited, Tanith forced food and drink down my throat—this was possibly the first time in my entire life I wasn't hungry—and explained how she'd chosen to change her name to Tanith, in honor of the Phoenician goddess of love and beauty. And dragons, apparently. She'd even tried to get me to sleep, but while I obediently lay down, my mind refused to shut off. The image of Inigo dropping dead at the hands of the Fairy Queen played over and over in my mind.

I felt a hand on mine. The procession of dragon kin had stopped in front of a pair of simple wooden doors. Tanith squeezed my fingers, and I sucked in a deep breath, forcing myself back into the present as the doors swung slowly open on creaky hinges.

The procession moved forward, and Tanith tugged on my hand. We passed through the doorway, two of the honor guard staying back to swing the doors shut behind us.

Here, the air was warmer, drier. The walls were smooth and shiny, as if the surface had been melted instead of rough hewn like the first part of the tunnel. It began to widen, from side to side and top to bottom, so the path was less like an alley and more like a broad avenue.

We moved deeper into the mountain, and I tried not to think of the tons of dirt and rock above my head just waiting to crush us all. I've never been a fan of underground places.

The top of the tunnel was so high, I could no longer make out the ceiling. The path curved left, and my eyes widened at the sight in front of us: two enormous doors, at least twenty feet high and coated in shimmering gold. Across the doors in bas relief was the image of a massive fire-breathing dragon.

***

Two of the honor guard peeled away from the rest of the group. Between one blink and the next, they'd shapeshifted into their dragon forms. It made sense. The only being strong enough to open those massive doors would be a dragon.

Each dragon grasped one of the rings in the center of a door with a claw and slowly pulled them open. Once again, we passed through a doorway, and once again the doors banged shut behind us. I ignored my lizard brain, which gibbered in fear. I was a guest of the dragons, their Fire Bringer. They would not harm me. As if sensing my thoughts, Tanith squeezed my hand again and gave me a sympathetic smile. I forced myself to focus on the fact that somehow this could all save Inigo.

At the head of the procession, Drago stopped in front of a small brazier. He carefully touched his torch to it. A flame sprang to life. For a moment, it danced there as if waiting, then it leaped, racing via a trough running along the outside wall of the massive cavern. More braziers sprang to life, one after the other, joining in the dance until the fire had nearly circled us, leaving only a narrow pathway through the flame.

I wondered vaguely why they didn't just use electricity like everyone else, but I was too overwhelmed by everything to focus on the mundane thought. My head felt hazy and full. It was all I could do not to fall to my knees and either cry my eyes out or beg the gods I didn't believe in to save Inigo.

The mellow light gleamed off row upon row of shiny stones inside the circle of fire. The enormous stones, each as big as a large man, were irregular in shape, but smooth and polished like the walls outside the gold doors. Unlike those walls, these stones shone in a myriad of colors, from deep rose to pale blue.

Drago turned and waved me forward. I glanced at Tanith, who gave me an encouraging nod. Sucking in a deep breath, I stepped past the long row of dragons still in their human forms and faced the Dragon King, brother of my beloved. Drago placed his hands on my shoulders and held my gaze. I read compassion in his eyes, and it made me want to weep.

"Morgan, this is the first time in centuries we have allowed a human to pass through the gates of our most sacred place. What you see here you must not tell anyone."

I nodded, swallowing the giant lump in my throat that was half sorrow and half trepidation. In the dancing light of the surrounding fires, Drago's golden eyes gleamed eerily. In that moment he was anything but human.

He squeezed my shoulders. "You must swear it, Morgan. Aloud."

"On my life?"

He shook his head. "On your Fire."

Inside me, the Fire woke up, straining against the bonds I'd placed on it. My hands trembled, and I clenched them into fists. Clearing my throat, I spoke loud enough for the entire gathering to hear. "I am Fire Bringer. On the Fire within me, I solemnly swear nothing I see within this sacred place shall pass from my lips." It was embarrassingly melodramatic, but I would have done anything for a chance to save Inigo.

Drago let go of my shoulders and beckoned me forward. I followed him past the first line of braziers and into the rows of stones. The others disappeared from view as he led me deeper into the cavern. There were dozens of stones. Maybe even hundreds. I squinted at the closest one, a pale pink with an undertone of gold. Had something moved inside? Surely not. That was impossible. Things didn't move inside rocks.

We finally stopped in front of the most beautiful of all the rocks I'd seen so far. It stood as high as my head and was perhaps four feet wide and equally deep. It shimmered in iridescent tones of peacock blue, green, and gold.

"This is gorgeous," I breathed. "What is it?" I held my hand out, not touching the stone, but close enough to feel the tingling energy radiating off it. I felt heat, as if a fire burned inside it. Startled, I glanced up at Drago.

"That is what your people call a dragon egg. Touch it."

Baffled, I laid my hand gently against the side of the rock. Except it wasn't a rock at all. The surface gave slightly beneath my hand, like one of those stress-relieving gel balls. The heat felt good. It was gentle and welcoming, and the Fire inside me basked in it, rolling around like a dog wanting its belly scratched. Could it be? Surely not.

I cleared my throat. "An egg? I thought dragons gave birth like humans do." Give me a little longer to pretend.

"We do," he said. "We are not born from eggs. We are reborn from them."

I blinked, still not wanting to accept the truth. Knowing I had no choice. "You mean…"

Drago placed his hand beside mine on the brightly colored egg. "Inside this egg is my brother and the man you love."

***

I jerked my hand back, staring at the egg in confusion and horror. "Inigo's in there?"

"Yes."

"How do we get him out?" I stepped toward the egg as if I would single-handedly rescue him.

Drago grabbed my arm. "We don't. This is how we heal our wounded. Even those near death have been known to recover."

Hope sprang up inside me. "This will heal him?"

Drago hesitated. "Maybe."

I whirled on him. "What do you mean, maybe? Will it heal him or won't it?"

"Morgan, please. I cannot answer what I do not know. Inigo was badly injured; he's a hairsbreadth from death. The egg is keeping him alive, but beyond that,"—he shook his head, a heavy line forming between his eyes—"we do not know. He is a halfling, and we have no idea if the egg can repair the damage. Or how long it will take."

I placed my hand against the egg once again, feeling the welcoming warmth. I tried to reach out somehow, to communicate. But it was Inigo who had the mind-speak, not me. I sensed nothing.

"What do you mean?" I spoke barely above a whisper, choked with tears, but Drago heard me.

"His injuries were extensive and, because of his human blood, he is more difficult to heal. If the egg works...it could take a long time."

I caught his gaze and held it, determined to wrangle the truth from him. "How long, Drago?"

This time the sympathy was like a dagger to my heart. The only thing that kept me upright was the egg beneath my hand.

"You'll be dead, Morgan," Drago said. "By the time the egg heals him, if it does, you'll have long been ashes and dust."

The bottom fell out of my world. And then a thread of hope. "Jack said I might be a Sunwalker," I whispered so low only Drago could hear me.

He squeezed my hand. "If that's true, you might have a chance."

Chapter 3

Heavy mist swirled around my feet, curling its way up my ankles to my calves. It was cool and cloying. I couldn't seem to find my way out of it. The more I pushed, the thicker the mist became. I couldn't see the ground beneath it, either, so I stepped cautiously, feeling my way along. No telling what was underneath.

A tendril slid across my face, sticky as a wet spider web. I slapped at it. There'd better not be any spiders hiding in the mist. Spiders freaked me out.

Ahead was a shimmering wall of white light dancing with sparkles of color. It stretched from one side to the other as far as the eye could see. I moved toward it. As I drew closer, I realized it wasn't a wall at all, but a curtain of energy more like a force field. How strange. It was warm and gave of a faint sound almost like a wind chime in a gentle breeze. The sparkles danced faster, like facets on a disco ball. I felt dizzy, disconnected from my body. I reached out to touch the wall, drawn by some force beyond myself.

"I wouldn't do that." The voice brought me back to myself with a crash.

I whirled around, startled. "Inigo? Oh my gods." I started to run toward him, but the mist grabbed at my ankles, holding me back.

Inigo gave me that adorable lopsided smile that flashed a perfect set of dimples. "Hi, Morgan."

"I miss you. Are you okay? How did you get here? Where are we?" Words spilled from me as I tried desperately to pull myself free from the mist and run to him. The harder I fought, the tighter it pulled

until it felt as though I was rooted to the spot. *"What the hell? Why can't I move?"*

"You can't touch me, Morgan. It's not safe."

I looked into his beautiful sapphire eyes and hot tears welled in my own. All I wanted to do was touch him. To know this was real. *"What do you mean? Why isn't it safe?"*

"You have to move on, sweetheart." His expression was sad, but his tone was firm.

"Move on? Are you nuts? I'm never giving up on you. Never. You are going to wake up." I didn't much care that Drago thought otherwise.

"Maybe. Someday. But by then, years will have passed. If you're still alive, you will be an old woman, and you will have wasted your life waiting. I will not let that happen." He gave me a fierce look. *"You will not waste your life on me, do you understand? You must forget me and move on."*

"No..."

"Move on, Morgan. Promise me."

"I won't." Had he faded a bit?

"Move on, or I will never have peace." He was definitely fading. Disappearing before my eyes.

"Wait, Inigo, don't go." I tried to reach out, but realized the mist had moved up, wrapping itself around my waist, my arms, holding me in place. *"Inigo!"*

"Forget me."

I woke up thrashing in bed, the blankets and sheets tangled tight around me and my face wet with tears. With a sob, I managed to free myself. The duvet, with its cheerful aqua and coral cover, slid to the floor. I didn't bother picking it up even though the coolness of the room made me shiver. It was no worse that the mist.

Without thinking of the time, I grabbed my cellphone and dialed Cordelia. It rang several times before my friend answered. She sounded half asleep.

"Cordy." It was all I could choke out past the sorrow that welled in my throat.

"Morgan? Is that you?" Sleep disappeared from her voice.

"Yes." A sob caught at my throat.

"Oh, my goodness, I haven't heard from you in weeks. Are you okay? What's wrong?"

"I had another dream." I'd had one nearly every night in the weeks since I'd left dragon land and Inigo's...egg. Each one was worse than the last, and each time, my heart broke a little more.

"Tell me." Cordy's tone was completely alert. No sign now I'd woken her from a dead sleep.

I told her about Inigo and the dream. Every detail I could remember. By the time I was finished, I felt like my heart was shattering all over again.

"Oh, Morgan," she whispered. "I'm so very sorry."

"What do I do?" I sobbed. "I can't let him go. I can't."

She was silent for a moment. "Listen to me carefully, Morgan. I know you put a lot of faith in your dreams, and that's good. They've shown you a lot. Dreams are important. But you must remember one very important rule: you can't always trust your dreams."

I frowned. "Why not?" So far my dreams had never led me wrong. They'd always been dead accurate, which was kind of scary, but also oddly comforting. Until now. This time, I hoped Cordy was right because beneath it all what I felt was fear and guilt. Fear that the dreams came from *me,* that part of me really wanted to just move on. Guilt, because I still wasn't over Jack.

"Because," Cordelia said softly. "Dreams can be meddled with."

***

The kitchen tile was cold against my bare feet. Despite the warm spring days, the nights were still chilly. I thought vaguely about grabbing a pair of socks from the bedroom, but didn't have the energy to move. So I stood there, feet freezing, staring out the window at the moonlit backyard.

After the dream and the chat with Cordy, I couldn't sleep. Par for the course these days. Ever since Inigo…

I shook off the memories. I wished I could shake off the soul biting sorrow as easily. And the hot tears that tightened my throat and threatened to spill over.

Cordelia hadn't been able to tell me much more about the dream manipulation. Part of me hoped she was right, because that would mean Inigo wasn't really telling me to move on. The problem with that was, if she was right, and Cordy usually was about such things, somebody was messing around with my head. I definitely did not like that idea. Still, if my amulet had meddled with my dreams in order to show me truth, why couldn't someone else meddle with them for another reason? Maybe a bad reason.

But who? And why?

Running a hand through my short hair, I turned on the faucet and splashed my face with cold water. I poured myself a glass of the stuff and chugged it down. The lump in my throat remained. I was getting used to it.

I fingered the amulet that hung around my neck. Sometimes I wished the thing had never chosen me.

I went back to bed, but sleep would not come. My brain kept churning until I wanted to scream in frustration. I sat up and braced my head in my hands, willing my mind to still.

No. The voice whispered through my head.

"What the hell?" I shook my head. Crazy. I was finally going batshit crazy for real.

Kill. Dark tendrils leaked out of their hiding place, wrapping themselves around my heart. *Kill.*

"This is insane. You are now officially certifiable." I guessed playing hermit for weeks on end had finally done what years of hunting hadn't.

Images flashed through my head. Visions of blood and death. My hand itched for a blade so I did what any hunter would do: I got up and threw on some clothes.

It was time to hunt.

Chapter 4

It was that time between night and dawn when everything was perfectly still. Even the birds were silent, as if the entire world was waiting to exhale. The ancients called it the hour of the wolf. I called it the hunting hour.

I parked my car in front of one of the enormous houses perched in the hills of Arlington Heights, near the International Rose Test Garden. This one looked like it belonged in an English forest. It even had the cottage garden to match. Technically, it was illegal to park here this time of night unless you were a resident, but Kabita didn't run a fake PI firm for nothing. I pulled a resident permit out of my glove box and stuck it in my front window.

My trunk held an entire arsenal of vampire hunting equipment: knives, swords, and a machete, not to mention UV guns and flash bangs. There was even a small bucket of salt and an old detergent bottle full of holy water, which, by the way, only worked on demons. I found myself staring at them, mind blank. Inside, the Darkness whispered. All these weapons made it too easy to hunt. Too easy to kill. I needed a challenge.

I nodded as if the Darkness could actually see me. I curled my hand around one of the simplest, most humble weapons I owned: a machete. Perfect for killing vampires. It would be all I hunted with tonight. Sliding the naked blade into the sheath strapped to my leg, I headed into the park.

The Rose Test Garden was the oldest of its kind in the entire United States. The purpose of the garden was to test new varieties of roses in our Pacific

Northwest climate. Those that survived were joined by hundreds of other varieties over the years. Acres of roses stretched out across the hillside, interspersed with walkways, statues, and water features set within miles of forested parkland. During the day, the place was crawling with tourists. At night, it was supposedly deserted.

Much like Pittock Mansion nearby, the Rose Test Garden with its sweeping views and heady scents was a hangout for daring lovers and stargazers. It wasn't like the place was fenced or guarded. Anyone could walk in at any time, and the vampires knew it.

I finally found a break in the line of tennis courts bordering the street and followed the narrow pathway between them. A long flight of concrete steps led down to the main parking lot, now barricaded until morning. From there, I took a second flight of concrete steps down into the gardens themselves.

The sweet smell of thousands of roses hit my nose. I inhaled, dragging their perfume into my lungs. For the first time in what seemed like forever, the tight ball of pain inside me relaxed.

I gave myself a mental slap. I didn't need to relax. I needed to hunt, to fight, to kill. Such thoughts should have given me pause, but instead I found my heart pounding with excitement as I hurried deeper into the gardens, eager for a fight.

A slight breeze kicked up, rustling the leaves all around me. I ignored the sound and the natural inclination to believe it meant something. Instead, I honed in on that other sense of mine, the one that told me when a vampire was near.

The amphitheater was the natural place to check first. With its wide grassy steps open to the sky, it was the perfect place to stargaze. Tonight, however, it was empty.

As I moved around the upper rim of the amphitheater, I felt that gripping at the back of my skull that told me a vampire lurked nearby. I paused to listen, trying to tune out the natural rustle of wind and foliage. There, just beyond the tall evergreens marking the back of the amphitheater stage. Voices.

I took the stairs down as quickly as I could without breaking something. Like my neck. Granted, I'd be more likely to survive the fall than a normal human, but it would hurt like hell.

The farther down I went, the tighter the gripping on my skull. Definitely getting closer.

The thick wall of evergreens ended before the edge of the hillside began. A narrow pathway wound between the trees, partially hidden by a low-hanging branch. I darted beneath the branch, into the grassy hideaway behind the stage, and stopped dead in my tracks.

Two faces stared up at me from a rather...compromising position. Clearly, the young men had thought this secluded section of the garden would make for a perfect trysting place. They hadn't counted on yours truly crashing the party. Nor had they counted on the vampire currently hiding in the bushes on the other side of the clearing. It must have seen me, though, because it took off down the hill with very little finesse and a whole lot of noise.

"Er, hi, boys. Just out for an evening stroll. Don't mind me." I scurried across the grass to the other side as quickly as possible, trying really hard not to stare at their rather spectacular physiques. "As you were." I gave an airy wave as I slipped into the bushes.

The minute I was out of sight, I broke into a full run. Well, as full a run as I could get while running headlong through rose bushes and other flora. The vampire was hella fast.

The waffle soles of my leather boots thudded against the hard ground as I hit the edge of the rose beds and plunged into the forested area below. Branches snagged at my leather jacket and swiped at my exposed skin. After a few hundred feet, I burst out onto one of the blacktop drives circling through the park. I saw a flash of movement farther down the road and took off after it. The vampire was headed toward one of the reservoirs.

A smiled tugged at my lips as I pushed myself a little faster. If the vamp thought it could hide underwater, it had another "think" coming. I happened to know that particular reservoir was empty for repairs.

Sure enough, the vampire paused at the edge of the reservoir and let out an angry howl. His hesitation allowed me to close the gap. Now I could tell it was a male, and a young one at that. No more than a year old. Maybe two. He looked kind of scrawny and malnourished.

With nowhere to go, he turned and snarled at me, curling his fingers into fists. Definitely new. Vampires didn't usually fist-fight.

"Hey, big boy," I taunted as I pulled my machete out of its sheath, the blade gleaming dully in the starlight. "Wanna dance?"

He hissed, his face twisting into an ugly parody of humanity. "That's fucking stupid. You been watching Schwarzenegger movies, bitch?"

"That's Miss Bitch to you, vampire. And don't you know better than to mock a hunter?"

His eyes widened. What? Had he honestly thought ordinary citizens ran around chasing vampires armed with machetes? Gods, what a newb.

He recovered his bravado quickly. "Whatever, bitch. No way you can take me on, hunter or not. You're just a dumb girl."

Was he serious? "Dumb I may be, but believe me, I'm all woman. I can kick your droopy ass any day of the week and twice on Sundays."

With a snarl, he launched himself at me. I darted to the side, and he hit the pavement with a sickening thud and a winded grunt. I raised my machete, but before I could bring it down on his neck I found myself on my back staring up at the stars. I hadn't even seen him move. Either I was getting slow, or I was letting my emotions get the better of me.

The boot came out of nowhere, nearly snapping a rib in two. It was my turn to grunt as I curled against the stabbing pain.

"That's what you get for messing with me, bitch." The boot lashed out again, but this time I was ready. The machete blade caught the vamp in the calf mid-kick. He let out a howl of pain as thick, dark blood oozed from the deep gash in his muscle and soaked through the leg of his jeans. "I'm gonna fucking *kill* you, bitch!"

He kicked my arm so hard, I heard the bone snap as the machete fell out of my useless fingers. I felt it too; the pain came so hard and fast, I'd have spewed my dinner all over the street if not for the fact I hadn't eaten in...well, I wasn't sure how long, but it had been awhile.

I tried to crawl away, but the vamp grabbed a handful of my hair, twisting until tears poured from my eyes. I was half surprised it didn't rip from my scalp. He dragged me along the ground, the asphalt scraping chunks out of my skin.

"You think you can take me on?" he was practically screaming. "I'll show you, you stupid bitch."

Gods, he was awfully fond of that word. I grabbed at his fist with my good hand, but it was useless. He was far too strong for me to fight one-handed. I needed to reset the bone in my arm so it could heal. Otherwise, I was screwed.

I suddenly realized a broken arm was the least of my worries as he jerked my head around so I could see where I was. He'd dragged me to the edge of the empty reservoir.

"See that, bitch? That's where I put hunter bitches." He seemed awfully pleased with himself.

"Yeah?" I managed to choke out past the pain. "You meet many hunter bitches? I bet not. Bet you'd wet your pants if you did."

With an angry scream, he moved to throw me into the reservoir to my death. Fortunately, he hadn't counted on two things. First, the sides of the reservoir curved slightly so if a person fell rather than got thrown, they'd sort of tumble and slide their way down. Second, I wasn't about to let some punk ass wannabe-badass fledgling vampire take me out. No, sir.

As he pushed me, I grabbed onto him as tight as I could with my good arm. He let out a girlish scream as we plunged over the side, tumbling over and over in what seemed like a never-ending fall.

Chapter 5

Halfway through the fall, with my lizard brain in full-on panic mode and body wracked with pain, the inner seal I kept on the Darkness ruptured. It roared out of me, my already-fuzzy vision narrowing to a pinpoint. We hit the bottom of the reservoir with a solid *thud*. Fortunately, I landed on top of the vamp. For all his scrawniness, he was still softer than concrete.

I vaguely registered my broken arm and possibly dislocated shoulder were now pain-free and working just fine. The Darkness had accelerated my healing process.

Sitting up, I braced my knees on either side of the vamp, straddling his waist. I stared down at his still form. Part of me registered how young he was. Hardly more than a teenager when he'd changed, poor kid. He hadn't had a chance. The larger part of me, the part the Darkness had taken, saw only its next victim. The vampire's eyelids fluttered. He was coming around.

I watched as my hands reached out, as though operated by a force other than myself. They grabbed the vamp on either side of his head. I willed them to let go, but I was no longer in control of my own body. The vamp thrashed against me, panicked. "No," he begged. "Please, no."

The Darkness didn't care. It smashed his head into the ground once, twice, three times. There was blood everywhere, splattered all over me, my clothes, and the side of the reservoir. Of course, the vamp wasn't dead. He just probably wished he was.

Blood burbled out of his mouth as he tried to speak. His hands pushed at me weakly. *Pathetic*, the Darkness whispered in my head. It wanted to play with him more, to make the victim feel more pain, to suffer.

"No," I shouted. "I won't let you do this."

But it's fun, the Darkness whined. *You want this.*

"I don't. I don't want this."

The vampire stared at me as if I'd lost my mind. He struggled, landing a solid blow to my cheekbone. Clearly, he was already healing.

The Darkness wrapped my hand around the vamp's throat and squeezed as if to crush his windpipe. Instead, the vamp landed another blow and then threw me off him. I hit the concrete floor of the reservoir and tumbled several feet until I hit the wall with a grunt. Pain lanced through my still-bruised ribs and tender arm.

The vampire jumped to his feet and turned to face me, triumph gleaming in his eyes. He rushed me, but I rolled to the side, kicking out to catch him across the shins. He toppled over in an ungainly heap. I gave him another good kick, hoping to catch him in the head, but it only glanced off his shoulder. Dammit.

He was up again before I was halfway to my feet, charging like an angry bull. The Darkness wanted to meet him head on, but I had a different plan. A split second before we connected, I dropped to one knee and hunched over. The vamp hit me like a freight train, his own momentum tossing him up and over my shoulder like a rag doll.

I won't lie. It hurt like hell. I was pretty sure I'd seriously strained my shoulder, but I didn't have time to stop for an assessment. At least it wasn't dislocated or anything, since I could still use it. More or less. I hauled myself up and staggered over to where the vamp was lying, stunned. He'd taken a header into the concrete and left quite a bit of skin behind. Blood poured from his nose. He started to get up, so I did the one thing I could think of: I sat on him.

He hit the ground face-first with a slight *oomph.* For some odd reason that made me feel vindicated.

"I'm sorry, big boy, but it's time to end this," I told him.

"Fuck off," he snarled.

I didn't answer. The Darkness was urging me to hurt him, make him suffer. It wanted me to pour out all the pain and rage inside me onto this one vampire. It was tempting, but I ignored it. Instead, I placed my palm flat against the vamp's back, over where his heart was. Then I let the Fire loose.

The Fire tore up and out from inside of me, where my powers lived. It surged through my skin, ripping down my arms and into my hands until I was a living flame. I felt heat, but the Fire didn't hurt me. I felt purified from the inside out.

Beneath me, the vampire screamed and writhed as the Fire burned through him and hit his heart. One moment he was a living, or rather unliving, creature, and the next, he was a pile of ashes surrounded by blood splatters.

I sank to one side as the Fire slowly made its way back inside me, taking the Darkness with it. I rolled over on my back, staring up at a sky that was just starting to lighten. Soon, visitors would pour into the gardens. My whole body throbbed with exhaustion and pain, and I was stuck at the bottom of a freaking reservoir for the whole world to see. Not to mention my machete was lying somewhere at the top. Crap.

I pulled my phone out of the inner pocket of my jacket. Kabita had recently given me one of those phone cases that looked like it belonged on a spaceship. I could pretty much drop my phone at the bottom of the sea or throw it in a volcano, and it would be fine.

Punching in Kabita's number, I listened to the other end ring. And ring. Finally she picked up.

"You better be dead. Do you know what time it is?" Her voice was scratchy with sleep.

"Not quite dead, but close. I've got a scene that needs cleaning."

"This couldn't wait until a decent hour?"

"By the time a decent hour rolls around, this place will be crawling with tourists," I said. "Can you imagine how we'd spin a giant blood pool and a lost machete?"

A long-suffering sigh. "Where are you? You sound like you're at the bottom of a well."

"Uh, yeah. I kind of am."

There was a pause on the other end. "Why me?"

***

"You smell like a dumpster."

"Gee, thanks. Good to see you, too." I scowled at Kabita, who was using a hand vac to suck up vampire dust.

"I'm serious. When was the last time you showered?"

I thought it over. "I honestly can't remember." I know, gross. But it wasn't like personal hygiene had been on my list of priorities.

Kabita turned off the vacuum and twisted her hair up in a bun. Then she pulled out a spray bottle and started spraying liquid over the bloodstains. The reek of bleach stung my nostrils. "You can't wallow and take a shower at the same time?"

"I am not wallowing."

Kabita paused her spraying and gave me The Look.

"Okay, maybe a little."

She sniffed delicately. "By the smell of it, a lot. You drown out the bleach."

That really was bad.

"And when was the last time you ate?"

I had to think about that, too. "Um, last night?"

"I mean something besides pints of chocolate and peanut butter gelato."

Damn. She knew me too well.

"That's what I thought." She nodded toward the ladder propped against the side of the reservoir. "Now you go home, get cleaned up, and eat some real food. I expect to see you in the office this afternoon."

I turned to go. I had no intention of going anywhere near the office. I gave a slight sniff. I might take a shower, though. Kabita was right. I smelled like a dumpster.

"And Morgan."

"Yeah?" I glanced back to see The Look had returned.

"If you don't get your shit together, I'm calling your mother."

Chapter 6

One month later.

I'd been to Nevada once before. Las Vegas, to be precise. The usual: gambling, drinking, dancing, male strippers, and way too little sleep. That had been back when I'd had a normal life, with a normal job and normal friends who had normal bachelorette parties.

This particular trip was anything but normal. But then, so was my life these days. I slid a sideways glance at Trevor Daly in the driver's seat of the government-issue SUV, his eyes shaded by mirrored sunglasses. Part of me wondered if this little adventure wasn't something Kabita and my half-brother had cooked up just to get me out of Portland for a while.

"Are you sure you're ready to do this? You don't have to, you know. I can handle it," he assured me for about the hundredth time.

"I know. I'm ready." More or less.

I turned my gaze back to the scenery, such as it was. The Nevada desert was just about as exciting as the one in Central Oregon. The dirt was red, the bushes half dead, and everything was dry as a bone. It was a lot warmer, though. Surprisingly so, for early March.

I knew he wasn't talking about the trip itself. It wasn't the trip that bothered me. It wasn't even the reason for the trip that bothered me. It was the fact that the body of the man I loved lay wrapped in a cocoon somewhere in a cave in Scotland, guarded by the Dragon King's men. Dead, but not dead. Just...mostly dead.

I knew dwelling on the situation would only send me on yet another downward spiral. I'd already spent enough time on that not-so-happy train. Even after a month of focusing on my job and pretending everything was hunky-dory, I was still perilously close to going over the edge. So I changed the subject.

There was something that had been bothering me ever since I'd dusted that soul vamp a few months ago, back before everything went to hell in a proverbial handbasket. I decided now was as good a time as any to bring it up.

"Trevor, have you ever seen a vampire with a soul?"

"Vamps aren't made with souls," he said, eyes glued to the road.

For a minute it didn't register, and then what he'd said hit me. "Does that mean a soul can be added later?"

He was quiet for a moment. "There are rumors," he finally admitted with some reluctance. "Nothing with any real substance to back it up, but I've heard that certain government scientists have been using necromages to experiment with vamps. Trying to control them. Still, this is the government we're talking about. Even if it is true, it'll take sixty years and ten-trillion dollars. I wouldn't worry about it too much."

"Why control?"

He glanced at me. "They make the perfect weapon."

I snorted. "They do not. Given the right conditions, that virus could spread like a wildfire."

The Atlantean virus that had created vampirism was highly contagious and totally unpredictable. It turned its host into a ravening beast and killed anything human that remained. I had no idea what happened to a person's soul when they got turned into a vampire, but under normal conditions, it just…left the building. I'd seen it happen. Once.

The government had never before taken an interest in the inner workings of a vampire other than as a disease to eradicate, a monster to destroy. They were far too dangerous to mess around with, otherwise.

"That's true," Trevor agreed, "Unless you're trying to spread it." His face was impassive behind his aviator sunglasses.

"What kind of an effing moron would do that?" It was insane. I mean, okay, I could see some lunatic in Congress or something thinking that setting a few vampires loose on our nation's enemies would be a clever idea. But it wasn't. Even if you could control the vampire, nobody could control the virus.

Trevor shot me an amused look. "Please, Morgan, people have done dumber things for the promise of power."

"But why put a soul in the vampire?"

"You need a soul to control them. The trouble is getting one and then getting it into the vampire."

I shot him a look. "Did you forget Brent Darroch? He controlled them without souls."

"And look how well that turned out. They were unpredictable at best, and he could only control them as long as he was in the same city."

"So putting a soul in them makes them less prone to crazy, and easier to control over distances?"

It made a scary sort of sense, and I did not like the thought of somebody running around shoving souls into vampires so they could...do what exactly?

"Theoretically. Like I said, it's only a rumor. Let's not forget why we're here."

As if I could forget that.

The road was blocked by a cyclone fence with a simple electric gate wide enough to let in a single car. Nothing fancy, nothing that shouted there was a top secret facility here. Except that next to the gate was a black Humvee, and next to it stood a man dressed in black, a nasty looking automatic weapon in his hand.

"Give me your passport and keep your hands visible," Trevor said, eyes on the man in black.

"Uh, okay." I handed Trevor the passport, then placed my hands on the dashboard in plain sight of the armed guard.

The guard waited until Trevor rolled down the window and flashed his Environmental Protection Agency badge. In reality Trevor worked for the SRA, the Supernatural Regulatory Agency. The SRA was a very secret agency operating under the umbrella of the Environmental Protection Agency. Their job was to oversee all matters pertaining to supernatural creatures and events, and they paid people like Kabita and me big bucks for our "special" talents.

Assured we were official, the guard carefully approached the car, ready to spray us with bullets should we make a misstep. It did not exactly inspire confidence.

I noticed movement on the other side of the Humvee. A second guard, also in black, approached the vehicle, his gun pointed straight at my head. Freaking fantastic.

The first guard was silent as he looked over Trevor's credentials and my passport. He gave me a hard look, then asked Trevor, "Who is she?"

"Hunter."

The guard nodded, handed back our paperwork, and then spoke quietly into the mic of one of those earpiece things you see special agents wearing on TV. Whatever he heard back must have been good. He signaled to the second guard. The two of them stepped away from the car, and the gate began to slide back with a great deal of shaking and squeaking. Once it was open fully, the first guard waved us through.

We passed through the gate and continued up the rough gravel road, the car kicking up a cloud of dust behind us. I was trying really hard to focus on the task at hand. Figuring out the inner workings of a crazy person's brain was enough to drive me loony, but it was better than dwelling on something over which I had zero control. Drago had said all we could do was wait. The question was, did I have enough time?

The past few weeks had passed in one long stretch of tension. So far, the Fairy Queen hadn't declared war on the djinn. In fact, she hadn't made an appearance of any kind, but I was worried it was only a matter of time. She was not the sort to let things go so easily. Yes, the Marid had killed Alberich to avenge Zip. Yes, Alberich had been nuts, not to mention evil. He'd tried to kill me multiple times. Yes, the Queen had basically manipulated me into a situation where her brother was sure to get killed.

Still, the sidhe were a law unto themselves, and I doubted the Queen saw it quite as logically as I did, especially after what she'd done to Inigo. I seriously doubted she would be satisfied taking the life of a half-dragon. Especially if Drago could bring him back. Worse, I was pretty sure I now owed her another favor for getting her brother killed, even if that was what she'd wanted in the first place. Shit.

She wasn't taking my calls. Even using her true name didn't work. Not a good sign. Probably, she knew how pissed I was, though "pissed" seemed too small a word. Not that my feelings, nor those of any human, concerned her overmuch. What really made me angry was there was nothing I could do to her. She was far beyond the touch of even my powers.

On top of that, we still didn't know who'd ordered the hit on me, or why. It certainly hadn't been Alberich, as I'd originally believed. Frankly, he wouldn't have thought me worth the time, and the website with the hit advertisement was still active, complete with a lovely new photo of me outside the motel in Madras where the body of a Supernatural Regulatory agent had been found after Alberich had him murdered. I couldn't figure out who had taken that photo. There hadn't been anyone in the parking lot except for Inigo, my brother, and me. There hadn't been any further attacks, either, but I figured it was only a matter of time before somebody decided to take a run at the bounty.

The good news was the junkie kid, Mikey, who had helped us solve the agent's murder, had kept his promise and called the counselor on the card I'd given him. She didn't handle such cases, but she'd sent him to a facility that did. By all accounts, he was doing well in recovery. He'd even cut his hair and changed his name to Mick. A new name for a new start. There was hope for him yet.

Which brought me full circle back to Inigo, because I wasn't sure there was hope there. Drago had done everything he could, but it could be years, even decades. If ever. It was the "ever" part that bothered me.

Trevor pulled up to a second checkpoint. There was no fence and no gate, just a guard shack hardly bigger than an outhouse. There was only one guard with a handgun, but I had the oddest feeling we were being watched from somewhere out on the desert. Trevor handed over his government ID and my passport once again, and we went through another round of "who is she" followed by more chatting via earpiece. The young guard waved us through.

We drove a short way up the gently sloping road. As we topped the rise, I saw grim concrete buildings laid out in a neat grid below us. Men and women in various military uniforms scurried to and fro on foot or in little golf carts.

I quickly shoved thoughts of Inigo to the back burner. There would be enough time for that later. Too much time.

"Welcome to Area 51." Trevor flashed me a grin.

"I can't believe I'm actually here." It was a little disappointing, to be honest. I'd imagined…I don't know what. Alien spaceships, maybe? Guards with ray guns and jet packs? "It's all so…normal." Or as normal as a military base ever got.

"What did you expect? Little green men?" Trevor laughed.

"Oh, excuse me. It's okay to believe in demons and vampires, but not aliens?"

"We've got enough crazy on Earth without worrying about crazies from other planets."

He made an excellent point. Still, I couldn't help but wish for more. I wasn't an *Ancient Aliens* fan for nothing.

As we pulled onto the base, a jeep zipped out from behind one of the large concrete buildings. The man driving was dressed in military fatigues. He gave us a wave, motioning Trevor to follow him.

About an hour later, we were finally sitting across from the reason we were there: Jade Vincent, former dragon hunter and full-time crazy person. Also, Alister Jones's "goddaughter" and secret weapon. And she wanted to talk.

Orange wasn't her color. Or maybe it was the lighting. She looked washed out and sallow, skinnier than I remembered. Her hair was still the same defiantly spiky, platinum blonde. Apparently Area 51 provided the inmates with the services of a hairdresser.

"Okay, Dara. We're here." Dara Boyd was Jade's real name. I hoped it would remind her who she was before she became a hunter: the girl who'd lived in a little flat in London with her girlfriend. A girl who'd been like any other girl before Alister Jones sank his twisted claws into her.

She didn't move so much as a muscle.

I sighed. "You wanted to speak to me. Speak."

"My name," she said, grating out each word, "is Jade. And I have something for you."

I blinked. "For me?"

She took a crumpled envelope from inside her jumpsuit and slid it across the table. The expression on her face could only be described as mocking. It gave me the heebie-jeebies.

I glanced down at the envelope, and my heart skipped a beat. I recognized the crest. It was that of the Jones family. I'd seen it in Alister's office in England. Inigo had a smaller copy in his living room, as did Kabita.

"How did you get this?"

She ignored me. Instead she crossed her arms over her chest and leaned back in her chair, the chains around her slender wrists clanking against the metal table. I knew without a doubt she wasn't going to answer me or anyone else. She'd done what she came for, and she wouldn't say another word.

Trevor nodded to the guards, who grabbed Jade and hauled her back down the hall, presumably to her cage or wherever they kept homicidal maniacs with hunter abilities. Frankly, I hoped she'd rot there. After what she'd done to Inigo, and the innocent lives she'd taken, she deserved no less.

"What's in the envelope?" Trevor asked.

I stared down at the thing lying on the table like it might bite me. Just looking at it gave me a bad feeling. I really, really did not want to open it.

Slowly, I lifted the flap and pulled out a piece of vellum. Rich. Expensive. Scrawled across the creamy sheet was a single line of unfamiliar handwriting:

Tick tock, little Hunter.

Chapter 7

We were halfway out the door, headed for the car, when the alarm sounded. The shrieking cacophony echoed off the cinderblock walls. The assault on my sensitive ears made me cringe as armed guards poured out of doorways and charged this way and that looking stern and purposeful. The door to the parking lot literally slammed shut in my face.

"What the hell?" I flattened myself against the wall as a group of soldiers charged past, weapons drawn.

"Lockdown. There's been an escape." Trevor's expression was grim as he grabbed my arm and pulled me away from the exit.

The timing was too perfect to be coincidental. We'd shown up, met with Jade, received a cryptic note and a splash of attitude, and then someone escaped? It didn't take a genius to figure that one out. And since Alister Jones hadn't been caught yet, that left only one other person insane enough and connected enough to pick this exact moment to escape. In fact, I'd bet a dozen chocolate donuts on it.

Trevor pulled me around the corner and into the guard booth overlooking the one entrance to the building. The door of the booth slammed behind us, cutting off the noise and chaos. Inside the booth it was quiet; a small, flashing red light the only warning. I breathed a sigh of relief.

"Commander, what's the status?" Trevor asked one of the two men hunched over the bank of monitors flickering with images of the compound.

The older of the two men wheeled around. There was a sheen of sweat on his upper lip and across his bald head. Clearly, he wasn't having a good day. "Agent Daly. I'm afraid I have some news your agency isn't going to like."

"Which one?"

The commander's expression was grim. "Prisoner X756."

Trevor closed his eyes and pinched the bridge of his nose. "Damn." He sounded resigned and not terribly surprised.

"Who's prisoner X756?" I asked, glancing from my brother to the commander and back again. I was pretty sure I already knew the answer.

It was the commander who finally spoke. "Brent Darroch."

***

To say the escape of Brent Darroch was a bad thing would be an understatement of epic proportions. Not only was the man a descendent of Atlantis, like I was (he'd almost killed me once because of it), he had a score to settle. I was the one who'd captured him, with a little help from my friends. Trevor was the one who'd put him behind bars.

Even worse? I'd taken the Heart of Atlantis from him. As far as he was concerned, that was an unforgivable sin. Never mind that I was the Key and as such, the Heart and its power belonged only to me.

Basically, Trevor and I now had great big bull's-eyes on our backs. Not exactly a comfortable feeling.

"How did he escape?" Trevor snapped, going into full-blown secret agent mode.

"We don't know," the commander replied grimly. "But believe me, I plan to find out." From his tone, I had no doubt heads would roll.

Trevor was with the SRA, the Supernatural Regulatory Agency, and as such outranked every civilian in the joint. I had no idea what protocol applied when military personnel were involved, but it was clear the commander was willing to keep him in the loop, if not outright defer to him.

I desperately wanted to start asking questions. Like, was Brent Darroch connected to Dara/Jade, and if so, how? Had either of them had any recent visitors? And how the hell could they allow a dangerous criminal to escape Area 51, of all places? But I was just a guest here. This was Trevor's show. It went against my nature, but I bit my tongue.

"Show me his cell."

The commander nodded. "I'll have someone take you." He barked an order into the mic of his earpiece, and then turned his attention back to the guy at the controls, completely ignoring us. I couldn't say I blamed him. Finding the prisoner took priority over anything else.

A couple minutes later, there was a knock at the door, and a soldier poked his head inside the booth. He didn't look a day over eighteen. His hazel eyes were wide and excited, and there was a flush riding high on his freckled cheekbones. At a guess, I'd say this was the first "action" he'd seen since boot camp.

"Reporting for duty, sir." There was a definite eagerness to his tone which both amused and worried me.

"Roberts. Good. Show these agents the cell where we kept Prisoner X756." The commander barely glanced up from the flickering screen.

"Yes, sir," Roberts barked, snapping off a salute his commander didn't see or acknowledge. "Agents, if you will follow me?"

I hurried to keep up with the men's longer strides as Roberts led us to a bank of elevators. The steel doors had been painted a bland gray, no doubt in order to blend with the unpainted concrete walls. Everything looked the same; a person could get lost around here.

Roberts waved us into the elevator and pushed a button. The doors slid shut, and the car began its smooth descent. There were no numbers to indicate which floors we were passing. I took a deep breath, trying to focus on anything but the layers of rock looming above us ready to fall on our heads at any moment.

"How deep are we going?" I asked the young soldier.

Roberts smiled at me, hazel eyes crinkling at the corners. "Deep."

The car came to a stop, and the doors slid open. I took in everything around me as we stepped out of the elevator. Beyond the shriek of the alarm, I couldn't hear much but the thud of boots and the shouts of soldiers as they ran through the base searching for the prisoner. That was the downside of super hearing; one loud sound had a tendency to overwhelm everything else.

My other senses, however, were still intact. On this level, everything had been painted white. Walls, floor, and ceiling all the same painfully bright white that made me want to pull out my sunglasses. The elevator bank had been left its natural steel color, polished to a high sheen. It was like something out of a '80s sci-fi movie.

Roberts stopped before another gleaming steel door. It had no knob or handle, only a biometric pad on the wall next to it. Roberts placed his palm flat against the pad and waited. A few seconds later, the door slid open, and he waved us through.

The room beyond wasn't what I expected. In fact, it wasn't a room at all, but more like an airlock. It was tiny, barely big enough for the three of us, and one wall was lined with small lockers. Opposite the door we'd just come through was a second door with a tiny portal window in it. I couldn't see what was beyond. The door behind us slid shut, cutting off the shriek of the alarm.

"Normally, you'd have to take off all your jewelry, belts, and whatnot, but since the cell is empty…" Roberts shrugged as if to say he didn't see the point. Thank gods, he wasn't one of those stickler-for-rules types.

There was another biometric pad next to the door with the porthole. Roberts placed his hand against the pad and then leaned forward to press his eye against what was obviously a retinal scanner. The door opened, and I caught a whiff of something astringent in the air: smoke, and under the smoke was the tang of burned plastic. My nose itched, and I covered a cough behind my hand. Wonderful. I so did not need my allergies going haywire.

As we stepped into the space beyond, my jaw dropped. We were in a cavernous room the same blinding white as the hallway. Suspended in the center of the room, and I mean center as in top to bottom and side to side, was a clear bubble about the size of my living room.

Well, not really a bubble. More like a dome with a flat bottom and a bubble top. It looked like it was made of unusually thick plastic, completely seamless except for small tubes attached to the top which were probably for ventilation and maybe things like food and water. I swear it was straight out of Star Trek. In the bottom of the bubble was a gaping hole, the sides blackened and melted.

"This is where we kept the prisoner." Roberts crossed his arms over his chest and stared up at the dome with a frown. His freckles stood out starkly in the harsh white light.

I stared up, wincing slightly at the crick in my neck. "Plastic?"

"Impenetrable plastene," Roberts corrected. "I don't really get the science, but it's supposed to be stronger than steel. Completely impervious to any known weapon."

"Clearly, somebody figured out a weapon that would work," Trevor said dryly, eyeing the melted sides of the hole.

"Yeah. The science geeks are probably freaking over that one." Roberts was clearly amused by the thought.

I stepped underneath the suspended dome and stared at the hole, my mind churning. Other than the bubble itself, the rest of the room was untouched. No sign that anyone had ever been there, or how Darroch had made it through the doors once he'd gotten out of the plastene cell.

"How would someone break in here?" Trevor voiced my thoughts.

"Technically, they can't, sir." Roberts's tone was almost apologetic. "We're hundreds of feet underground and you'd need authorization to get in. Maybe you could tunnel your way underground if you had a *lot* of time on your hands. Use dynamite or something to blow your way through the concrete, but the walls haven't been breached."

"Someone hacked into the system, maybe?" I suggested.

"No, ma'am. No sign the system was hacked."

"You're telling me someone with authorization came in here and broke Darroch out?" Trevor snapped. His patience was obviously wearing thin.

"There's no record of anyone entering the chamber, sir." Roberts shook his head. "Not at that time, and not for hours before. There's nothing on the security cameras, either. One minute the prisoner was there, and the next he was gone."

"No one broke him out, Trevor," I interrupted, still staring at the hole above my head. "The burn marks are on the inside. Darroch cut himself out."

***

"Heads are going to roll." Trevor's knuckles were white as he gripped the steering wheel, a dark flush staining his cheeks. "The boss isn't going to like this."

The anger rolled off him in waves so strong I could physically feel it. I totally got it, though. I sure wouldn't want to be the one to tell his boss a top priority prisoner, one with very powerful and very evil connections, had escaped from an impenetrable cell. And from the inside, no less.

Despite scouring the base from top to bottom, there'd been no sign of anyone entering or exiting the building. Not even Darroch. It was like he'd vanished into thin air. I could smell hinky all over this thing.

"Holy crap, that's it."

Trevor glanced at me. "What's it?"

"He vanished into thin air."

"Uh, yeah." He gave me an eye roll. "That's the problem."

"No," I said, shaking my head. "I mean he literally vanished into thin air. That's why nobody saw him leave through the door. He didn't. Once he was out of that bubble, somebody zapped him out."

"Like teleportation, you mean?"

"Something like that, yes. It has to be."

He frowned. "As far as I know, Darroch doesn't have any such capabilities."

"He doesn't." I knew that from experience. He was batshit crazy in a power hungry way, and he was stronger than your average human. Smarter, too. But he didn't have superpowers. "But there are those that do." The Fairy Queen came to mind, with her tendency to yank me into the Other World whenever she wanted.

Trevor shook his head. "The alarm systems would have detected any sort of technology. There's no way he could have got a weapon in with him, let alone one that could open the dome."

I mulled it over. "Maybe somebody teleported one in?" I wasn't sure we were on the right track with the whole teleportation of weapons thing, but it was the best idea I had at the moment.

"Why not just teleport him straight out of the cell?" Trevor asked

Fair point. "Might have taken too much energy. A material strong enough to be impenetrable to any known weapon can probably dampen most extra-human abilities." I glanced at Trevor for confirmation, but his face gave nothing away. Good enough. "So, whoever it was teleported the weapon into the cell so he could cut himself free. Once Darroch was out, it was easy enough to teleport him through concrete walls, no matter how thick."

"Makes sense, I guess." Trevor still sounded doubtful. "So you know anyone with that ability?"

"Not really," I admitted. "Djinn can do it. Sidhe, too, probably. But I can't think of anyone I know personally who would give a crap about Brent Darroch. There are certain demons, of course, but they don't generally have any reason to get involved with humans other than for killing." I frowned. Something was niggling at the back of my brain. "It's odd, though."

"What is?"

"Jade was the one who called us to Area 51. Jade gave us the note."

"Jade has no connection to Darroch as far as I've been able to ascertain."

"She doesn't," I said. "But there's someone who might."

Our gazes locked, and I saw the moment the thought hit Trevor's brain. "Crap. Alister Jones. But he doesn't have any sort of psychic or telekinetic abilities."

"No, he doesn't." My tone was grim. "But Alister Jones has connections in very low places."

Chapter 8

It was raining when Trevor dropped me off at home; that steady, constant light rain Portland is known for. My lightweight jacket was waterproof, but the rest of me was soaked. Frankly, I couldn't have cared less.

The entire flight home on the SRA's private plane, I'd been turning Darroch's escape over and over in my mind. It was painfully obvious the whole thing with Jade had been Alister's idea of a joke, a way to prove he had the upper hand. But beyond that, I didn't have a clue why Alister Jones or anyone else would help Darroch escape Area 51. But while I chewed on the latest mystery, the Darkness had once again started up its insistent chant.

Hunt. Kill. Hunt. Kill. I'd told it to shut up, but it only laughed. The closer we got to Portland, the more insistent it became. Now that I stood at my back door, keys in hand, it was suddenly overwhelming.

I spun on my heel and marched to the car. A hunt would burn off some of this excess energy. Help me think more clearly.

I guess I was feeling reckless, because I was only wearing two of my usual blades. Lately, I had been giving my powers a lot more free rein. Those things that lived inside me, always wanting out. Well, tonight, I'd let them. I didn't care how dangerous it was. I didn't even care if they took over. I just wanted to fight and forget everything else for awhile.

As I pulled my car out of the drive, I forced myself to focus on the hunt. If I let my mind wander, it would go to maudlin places. That was the last thing I needed.

I was only two blocks from the house when I realized I was being followed. Maybe I was being paranoid. After all, plenty of people drive the streets of Portland at night for various reasons. But there hadn't been any cars on my street other than parked ones, and the lights suddenly flashing in my rearview mirror were too much of a coincidence to my already overly-suspicious brain. Besides, every instinct I had was screaming at me.

I'd learned a long time ago not to ignore my gut. I wasn't about to stop listening now, especially with a bounty on my head and Brent Darroch on the loose. Could he be after me already?

I was going the speed limit, which was twenty-five, so I took the next right without slowing down. Pressing down on the gas, I sped up a bit before careening around the next corner. The car was still on my ass. I was definitely being followed, and by someone who had no idea what subtlety was.

Hawthorne Street was nearly deserted, which was a good thing. The speedometer told me I was going fifty as I blew through a red light. Crossing my fingers that there weren't any cops around, I sped up the hill toward Mt. Tabor. It hadn't been my original destination, but it seemed like the best place to get away from everyone and take care of business.

The other car was hot on my tail as I cut left onto 60th and then right onto Reservoir. A hard left, and I was circling the park that covered the top of the hill. I slid to a stop in a small tree-lined parking lot with a squeal of tires and was out of the car almost before it stopped rolling.

The other driver jammed on his brakes, nearly sending his car into a tailspin. He managed to correct before he crashed his vehicle into mine. The guy was one hell of a driver.

The car was black and sleek and powerful. It looked like a Mercedes, but someone had removed everything from the license plates to the little icon doodad that usually sat on the hood. I guess I wasn't the only paranoid one. Even with my more than human night vision, I couldn't see into the interior, thanks to the tinted windows. Totally illegal in Multnomah County, but I doubted the driver was worried about getting a ticket.

I expected him to come charging out, but nothing happened. He just sat there. What was he waiting for? An engraved invitation?

"You going to sit there like a bump on a log all night?" Patience has never been my strong suit.

The driver's side door swung open and someone slowly stepped out. At first I couldn't make him out, thanks to the glare of the headlights, but then he stepped into the beams so I could see.

Immediately I could see my mistake. I admit it's sexist, but I see somebody with mad car skills like that and I automatically think "male." This driver was the exception. From her long blonde hair to her six-inch fuck-me heels, this driver was all woman. The cold expression in her eyes told me her skill set included something far more deadly than good driving.

"Well, now, is that any way for a lady to behave?" I taunted, trying to get a rise out of her. Keep your enemy off-guard, and they make mistakes. Mistakes that can save your ass.

It worked. She bared her teeth at me in a snarl, and my blood ran cold at the sight of long, sharp canines.

She might be all woman, but she was far from human. I should have sensed her, as I did all vampires, but with the combination of lack of sleep and adrenaline overload, my Spidey senses were off kilter.

"Let me guess." My tone was dry. "You're after the bounty." I still had no idea who had put a price on my head, but she was the second vamp who'd shown up planning to claim the prize, thanks to that stupid website.

She tilted her head to the side like a bird studying a bug. A slight smile curved her lips, and she gave her hair a flirty little toss, but her eyes remained cold and dead. "Mama needs a new pair of shoes."

I rolled my eyes. Fantastic. A vamp with a sense of humor. "You know you're not the first, right?"

"I don't imagine I am. But I will be the last." She evidently didn't suffer from lack of confidence.

My fingers closed around the handle of my *skean dhu* as I pulled it slowly from its sheath on my belt. The deadly little Scottish blade was the latest addition to my arsenal, and I was looking forward to giving it a workout.

I shot her my best "fuck you" smile. "Good luck with that."

Chapter 9

The vamp moved so fast my eyes almost couldn't track her. One minute she was standing there in skintight leather and a cocky attitude, the next, she was nothing but a blur. How she moved so fast in six-inch stilettos, I'll never know. I'd have broken an ankle for sure.

I had just enough time to crouch slightly and twist to the left before she slammed into me. The angle of my body threw her off balance enough to stagger her a little. I helped her along with a quick twist back to the right as I stood, flipping her over my shoulder. Instead of taking us both to the ground, she found herself flat on her back on the gravel, gaping like a fish. Sometimes I really love the laws of physics.

She growled low in her throat, an expression of pure rage crossing her perfect, icy features. She didn't have the usual slavering half-crazed vampire thing going on, which was odd, but I didn't have time to focus on that. With one smooth move, she was on her feet again, circling me like an angry dog.

"Is that all you've got?" I taunted as I stood my ground, blade in hand. "You're giving us girls a bad name, you know."

Her lips peeled back in a snarl, exposing her long, brutally sharp canines. "We should have exterminated you hunters generations ago. You're nothing but a pain in the ass." There was bitterness to her tone which spoke of more than a vampire's rage. This wasn't about a bounty, and it wasn't about blood. This was personal.

"What did we ever do to you?" As if I had to ask. No doubt one of us had killed her maker or something else within the realm the hunter's job.

"As if I would tell the likes of you," she hissed.

Whatever. I couldn't care less if she told me. I shrugged, using the movement to mask my true intentions as I braced myself for the throw.

The knife flew from my fingers, embedding itself in her eye socket. The vamp fell to her knees with a shriek of agony, her fingers clamping around the hilt of the knife.

A quick pounce, and I was on her, giving the blade a vicious twist before yanking it out in a gush of dark blood and yellow fluid. The ruined eye plopped out onto her cheek, held there only by the optic nerve. So much for icy beauty.

Her scream nearly deafened me, and the blood and eye goo made the *skean dhu* slippery in my hand. I tried for her throat, but my hand slid, the point of the blade grazing skin and glancing off her collar bone without doing any real damage. Enraged, she gave me a push, heaving me off her so hard I flew several feet across the parking lot. My head connected with the side of my car with a sickening thud, the knife skittering away under the vehicle. The pain and resulting nausea was instantaneous; I had barely enough time to lean to the side before I heaved up what little was in my stomach. Gods, this was the second time I'd lost my lunch during a fight. Good thing I hadn't been eating much lately.

That gave vamp lady enough time to get to her feet. She towered over me, her good eye snapping with anger, hatred, and something else. Something I'd seen once before.

Holy shit, the vamp had a soul.

"So, this is the mighty hunter of Portland, Oregon?" she taunted, her red-painted lips turned into an unattractive snarl. "What a pathetic little piece of trash."

She gave me a swift kick in the gut with her stiletto, which only served to make me puke again. I lay there completely helpless as wave after wave of dry heaves drained me of strength and left me vulnerable.

With a snort of what sounded like disgust, she squatted down next to me and grabbed a handful of my hair, yanking back my head so she could see my face. "Are you finished?" Yep, definitely disgust.

My voice was scratchy and raw, and I swear there were two of her swimming around in front of me. "Not hardly."

With one smooth move, I slid my second blade from my boot and thrust it into her abdomen just about where her diaphragm should be. She stared at me in shock as I ripped the blade downward, using the weight of my body to force the blade through muscle and sinew. With my strength nearly gone, gravity and body weight was all I had left.

Blood bubbled from her lips as she fell to her knees in the gravel. She stared in horror as her innards spilled out, glistening black in the glow of the headlights. She tried to stuff her guts back where they belonged, but I'd done too much damage. A stab wound was one thing, but once the insides were out, there was no coming back. The skin might heal over the mess, but the vamp would be trapped inside a non-functioning body. Nasty. Plus, I'd perforated something vital because the stench was nauseating. If I hadn't already puked my guts out from the blinding headache, the smell would have done it.

"Bitch…" It was hardly more than a whisper, but there was so much anger behind it, I might have been frightened if I'd been thinking straight.

I sank to the ground, my strength completely depleted. I stared up at her as her blood and other gunk poured over me, my knife blade still buried in her belly. I felt the Darkness that lived inside me raise its head. It liked causing pain, and I was causing vamp lady a lot of pain. In my current condition, there was no way I could control the Darkness, so I had to make this fast. I had one question. "Who gave you a soul?"

"Bitch…" Stronger this time. "I'm going to kill you."

"I doubt it. Now answer my question." I gritted my teeth against the throb of pain in my head, reached over, and gave the knife a vicious twist.

She shrieked in agony, trying to pull my hands away from the knife, but she was as weak as I was. "Fuck you." It was less a snarl and more a whimper.

"No, thanks." I turned the knife again, eliciting another cry. "You're not my type. Now tell me. Who did this?" The Darkness was surging. I had seconds at best.

She looked me right in the eye. I could see it all there…the pain, the suffering, the anger. Even the need for revenge. And, yes, I could see her soul.

"Fuck. You." She practically spat it.

The Darkness broke free, and the whole world tunneled down, narrow and dark. I watched my hand rip the blade from the vamp's belly, and then slash it across her throat in one fluid movement. My hand plunged the knife into her chest, punching though tissue, past bone, until it reached the heart.

Her eyes widened, and in a split second, she was so much dust, slowly sifting to the ground. The knife clattered from my numb fingers as the Darkness threw my head back and howled at the moon.

Chapter 10

I came to with my cheek pressed against the rough gravel next to my car. I had no idea how much time had passed, but I was chilled to the bone. My cheek was scraped raw from where a particularly pointy rock was poking it, and my head still hurt like hell. I tried to move, but the throbbing pain sent my stomach heaving again.

There was no way I could drive like this. Heck, I couldn't even get myself off the ground. And what about vamp lady's car? It was still there, one door wide open, motor running and headlights on. I couldn't leave it like that. Someone would see it and report it to the cops. Which would be fine except there was blood everywhere, including on me. It looked as if I'd survived a massacre.

My lips twisted wryly. Not far from the truth.

I managed to wiggle my phone out of my pocket without causing my head too much agony. The numbers swam in front of my eyes as I squinted at the screen. Finally I gave up trying to figure out the time. It was still dark.

I considered my options. Kabita had already had to clean up after me once. She would read me the riot act and then march my ass to the nearest hospital, which probably wasn't a bad idea based on how I was feeling. Jack would bitch at me and give me a bigger headache. Trevor? Well, what was family for if not to rescue your sorry ass in the middle of the night? Plus his contacts could get the "crime scene" covered up in no time, faster than even Kabita could manage. Perfect.

Unfortunately, actually dialing his number was another matter. I couldn't focus on the screen well enough to make out names. My fingers were numb and fumbly. I could hardly scroll through my contacts list. Shit. I really needed to get one of those phones that talked back.

I finally gave up and stabbed at a random contact. All I could do was hope I hadn't chosen my mother.

***

Chill wind lashed at my clothes and hair. I tasted salt in the air and the scent of sea teased my nose as I inhaled deeply. The bleak landscape was bathed in the sliver glow of the swollen moon overhead.

She stood at the edge of the cliff, her simple shift dress soaked from the spray of the ocean. Around her body I could see the glow of her inner fire. She was burning from the inside out.

I knew this place. This dream. I'd had it before. Only that time I'd been the girl...Fina, a creature of rage and fire, the Fire that lived inside me now.

I knew she burned with hunger. To devour, destroy. I knew because I'd felt it within me, and it scared me to death.

Below, the sea crashed against the jagged black rocks, sending another icy spray over her. It sizzled against her skin like oil on a hot stove, evaporating in seconds. She didn't notice.

"Fina! Fina!"

This time, I was the one who called to her, not the

boy. The moon child, Iah, was nowhere to be seen. Even the temple that was supposed to stand on the hill behind us had vanished. It was just the two of us, the rocks, and the sea.

The girl stepped closer to the edge of the cliff.

"Fina, please," I begged. My heart ached for her and for the boy she loved. It wasn't fair. "It doesn't have to be this way." After all, I'd survived with the Fire inside me. So far, anyway. Why couldn't she?

She didn't answer. Instead she stared out to sea, her body rigid as the wind plastered pale pink robes to her slender form. Her long red curls danced madly on the wind.

"You have to listen to me." My voice was hardly above a whisper, yet I knew she heard me. "What will Iah do without you?"

Still she ignored me. I knew it was only a dream, but somehow I wanted to change things. Wanted to make sure it turned out differently this time.

"What can I do, Fina?"

She turned to me, her face a pale mask. Her eyes were living flames. Terrifying. My heart raced in my chest as she held out cupped hands to me, each one filled with rich, loamy earth. The dirt trickled between her fingers as she stared at me, her eyes burning hotter with each second.

"Fire burns," she whispered. The glow around her intensified, so bright it made my head throb. I had to close my eyes against the light. "Earth cleanses..."

Chapter 11

My head felt like somebody had used it for batting practice. With every beat of my heart, a throb of pain made my stomach roil. I didn't want to open my eyes, but someone kept yakking at me.

I wanted to tell whoever it was to shut up, but my mouth refused to connect to my brain. I inhaled and tried again. "Go 'way," I mumbled. It came out a lot whinier than I'd intended.

"Not until you open your eyes." Kabita's tone brooked no argument.

I mumbled something rude.

"The same to you. Now open your eyes, or I'll open them for you."

I cracked open an eyelid only to have the light stab viciously at my eye. Pain was a hot poker in my brain. I hissed and tried to block out the light with my hand. I was only moderately successful.

I was in the hospital in what looked like a private room. Not that I was impressed. The mattress was too thin, and my back ached from lying in one position too long. The walls and floors were too white, the florescent lighting too harsh. It was clinical and cold as hell. The only colorful spot in the room was a really ugly painting of a vase of flowers which somebody with very poor taste had thought was a good idea.

I turned slightly toward my visitor, careful not to jar my throbbing head. Kabita Jones, best friend and boss, let out a sigh as she dragged a metal chair next to the bed and sank down on it. I closed my eyes again as she propped her feet on the mattress next to me. "You really do know how to cause trouble, don't you?"

I winced. "Keep your voice down. You're hurting my head."

"Well, at least you're alive."

Gods, I almost wished I wasn't. The pain was intense. I kept my eyes shut against the light. "Tell me you didn't call my mother."

"I didn't call your mother."

"Liar."

"You're in the hospital, Morgan," she snapped. "I had no idea how bad it was, but it didn't look good. At all." She sounded worried. And if Kabita was worried, I knew I was a hot mess. "Of course I called your mother. "

Great. Just great. All I needed was my mother hovering over me, listing everything I was doing wrong with my life, up to and including my choice of career. Granted, she thought I was a night manager at a local hotel, but I doubt she would have found vampire hunter a suitable occupation, either.

I swallowed. My throat felt like it had been given a good scrubbing with sandpaper. I opened one eye a slit, hissing against the sharp light. Unless she was hiding in the bathroom, my mother was nowhere to be seen.

"Where is she?"

"I sent her to get a cup of coffee. She was…stressed."

I would have laughed if my head hadn't hurt so badly. "Stressed" was no doubt an understatement. And, knowing my mother, she wasn't the stressed one. She was the causer of stress.

"Besides," Kabita continued, "we need to talk." Her face was expressionless, which didn't bode well.

Frak. Just what I needed. I sighed, closing my eyes again. "Listen, I'm not really up for a convo right now…"

"Don't care what you're up for," she snapped. Her boots hit the floor with a solid *thunk*. "I'm done with this death wish you've got going."

This time, I cracked open both eyes despite the pain hammering at the inside of my skull. Kabita's jaw was clenched, her silky dark brows drawn together in a frown. Man, she was pissed. "What are you talking about?"

"Ever since Inigo got…injured, you've been acting nuts."

Injured. That was one way to put it.

"Nuts?" I thought I'd done a pretty good job playing normal the last few weeks.

"First, you don't eat for months on end."

Kabita was totally exaggerating. Besides, it wasn't like a couple months without food would hurt me. There were enough donuts on these hips to insure survival through any famine.

"Next thing I know, you're calling me to rescue you from the bottom of a reservoir."

She made a fair point there. Although the whole "bottom of the reservoir thing" hadn't entirely been my fault.

"Then you take off for goddess-knows-where and end up in the middle of a prison riot," she continued.

"Okay, that part isn't exactly true. There was no riot."

She ignored me. "And then you manage to nearly get wasted in a parking lot. I know you're attacking random vampires, trying to get yourself killed."

"First, I was not *trying* to get myself killed. The vampire attacked me. Second, that's my job."

Kabita leaned forward, right into my face, her expression so fierce it was actually a little bit scary. "You went out there with nothing but a little bitty cooking knife and a boot dagger. What else am I supposed to think? You've gone off the frigging deep end, and I've had enough."

Damn. And here I thought I'd been hiding it so well. "So, what? You're firing me?"

She looked surprised at that. Her chair squeaked a bit as she sank back and crossed one jean clad leg over the other. "Of course not. Don't be stupid. Oh, too late."

I tried to scowl at her, but it gave me a worse headache than I already had, so I ignored the jab. "Then what?"

I swear to gods, Kabita smirked. "I'm sending you somewhere you can't hurt yourself. With someone who can force you to deal with your issues in a healthy way."

I blinked. She sounded like my cousin, the therapist. "What the hell are you talking about?"

Kabita gave me one of her enigmatic smiles and crossed her arms, feet back up on the bed. She was nothing if not smug.

"Come on, Kabita. Who did you call?"

"Me."

In the doorway stood an old man dressed in faded blue jeans and a matching shirt. His long white hair was tied back in a thick braid and his dark eyes sparkled with good humor and the mysteries of the universe. I'd know him anywhere.

"Tommy!"

***

Though they never met in life, Tommy Waheneka had been my father's friend. He was a shaman, a respected elder of the Warm Springs Confederated Tribes, and also my brother's guardian angel of sorts. If you looked up the word "enigmatic" in the dictionary, I'm pretty sure you'd find Tommy's weathered features staring back at you.

Tommy pulled a flask out of his back pocket and handed it to me. "This will help."

I was pretty sure booze wouldn't help a concussion, but I whispered, "Thanks," and unscrewed the cap. After the first sip, I knew it wasn't alcohol. I almost spit the vile stuff out. It tasted like goat bowel stewed in ditch water. Not that I'd know what either of those things tasted like.

"Are you trying to kill me?"

Kabita smirked again, but Tommy's face remained stoic, as usual. "Drink it all." His tone did not invite argument.

With a sigh, I held my breath and swallowed the stuff as fast as I could. There was a bit of gagging involved, and my eyes watered, but I got it down, followed by a full glass of water. Unfortunately, my mouth still tasted of goat bowel.

"Now what?"

He sat down in a chair next to the door. "We wait."

The silence was a thick, suffocating blanket. I could tell Kabita was still pissed at me. Tommy was unreadable. My head was still throbbing and my stomach still rioting. The antiseptic stench of the hospital didn't help matters any.

The *clip-clop* of sensible heels echoed in the hallway. Oh, gods. I'd know that sound anywhere.

My mother appeared in the doorway, a gently steaming paper cup in each hand. "Morgan! You're awake." She hurried to the bed, thrusting one of the cups at Kabita on her way. She set the other one down on the nightstand next to the bed and took my hands in hers. She looked pale and tired, her features drawn. I suddenly felt bad. She gave my hands a little squeeze. "How are you feeling?"

"Like hell."

"Language," she snapped, like I was a five-year-old.

"Sorry, Mom."

Kabita sat up, removing her feet from the bed so my mother could settle down next to me. The movement jarred my head, but the pain wasn't so bad this time.

My mother sat primly on the edge of the bed, smoothing her beige skirt over her thighs. She was perfectly dressed and coiffed, down to the pearls around her neck and the carefully applied lipstick in just the right shade of mauve. I detected the faint hint of Chanel No. 5 as she reached up to brush a lock of hair off my forehead. Even visiting her daughter in the hospital, my mother insisted on keeping up appearances. "I told you working the night shift was dangerous. I hope you've learned your lesson and you'll see about getting a decent, respectable position."

I must have looked completely blank, because my mother heaved a deep sigh. I had always been something of a trial to her.

"Sorry, Mrs. Bailey, but she's a little fuzzy about what happened," Kabita spoke up, sending me a sly wink. "Get a bash on the head like that, and you're bound to forget a few things."

"Oh, my." My mother looked horrified as she turned to Kabita, her face pale under her flawlessly applied makeup. "I saw that on Oprah once. People who've been violently attacked often suffer from amnesia and PTSD. You don't suppose Morgan will have PTSD, do you?" She turned back to me. "Does your insurance plan cover counseling? Don't worry. I'm sure your cousin will give you a free mental health assessment at the very least."

I opened my mouth, but nothing came out. I had no idea what to say. What on earth had Kabita told my mother? "Mom," I finally managed, "Jeanne is family. Assessing my mental health would be unethical."

"Well, that's ridiculous." Mom mulled it over. "My friend, Margery, has an excellent therapist. I'm sure he can give you a discount."

"Um, great." I happened to know Mom's friend, Margery, was sleeping with her therapist. I wasn't about to tell Mom that, though.

I shot Kabita a glare. She smiled blissfully and sipped her coffee. Tommy sat quietly next to the door, completely ignoring the whole scene. I wasn't sure, but I thought he might be meditating. That, or he was sleeping with his eyes open. Either one was entirely possible.

"Those horrible, horrible thugs, mugging you like that." Mom shook her head. "What is this world coming to? Your grandmother keeps saying this is the end times. Maybe she's right. All this violence."

My grandmother was a religious nut who listened to too many talk shows on the radio. If there was a conspiracy wackjob out there, she was probably listening to him or her. I remember my grandmother once declaring barcodes were the mark of the Beast and a sign of the end times, despite the fact that barcodes had been around for ages.

"Listen, Mom, stop worrying," I cut her off before she started quoting Revelations or something. "I'm not going to get PTSD." Mostly because I pretty much already had it, thanks to the vampire attack that had woken my hunter abilities. "I've just got a little concussion. I'll be fine." At least, I hoped I would. The headache was nearly gone now and my stomach no longer felt like it wanted to jump out of my throat. Whatever had been in Tommy's flask was starting to work its magic. Even I couldn't heal quite that fast.

My mother took a sip of her coffee, as if trying to steady herself. "You'll come home with me. I'll take care of you until you get better."

Oh, good lord. That was the last thing I needed. "Thanks, Mom, but I'll be fine. I'm, um, going on vacation."

That surprised her. She fidgeted with her pearls. "You are? When?"

"Well, I was going to go next month." Total lie. "But since I'm sure the doctor will probably tell me to take time off, I figured I'd go early. I'm sure I can change my reservations." I crossed my fingers under the blankets and noticed Tommy was grinning ever so slightly.

"But…but where are you going?" The fidgeting grew more pronounced. I knew if I told her I was going somewhere nice like Hawaii or Puerto Vallerta, she'd want to come. So I picked somewhere she'd never touch with a ten-foot pole. "Central Oregon." It wasn't a lie. Tommy's house was on the Warm Springs Reservation, and reservation land was just on the other side of Mt. Hood in Central Oregon.

She frowned. "Sun River? That's a nice place. Maybe I can go…"

"No. Not Sun River." Damn. I'd forgotten about that. Sun River was a very nice resort community. Biking, hiking, shopping, and restaurants. I was pretty sure there was even a spa. Just my mother's cup of tea. "I was thinking somewhere more…remote. Get away from it all. No phones or computers. No indoor plumbing. Just me and nature." Yeah, because I loved nature so much. I'd rather poke my eye out with a spork than "get back to nature."

My mother looked revolted, just like I'd known she would. "I'm sure you'll have a nice time, dear. But you probably shouldn't drive."

"Don't worry, Mom. I've got it covered."

I swear Tommy winked at me.

Chapter 12

At some point in the afternoon, I drifted off again. Thanks to my hunter healing ability, and whatever herbal magic had been in Tommy's flask, I was feeling better, but my head still ached and the meds made me drowsy. I was in that happy place between dreaming and waking, where the world just sort of floats gently around you, everything warm and cozy, when I felt someone standing next to my bed. Maybe if I pretended to be asleep, they'd go away.

"Welcome back."

Crap. Jack. I so did not want to deal with him right now.

I opened my eyes to see him sitting in the chair Kabita had vacated earlier. His long legs were stretched out in front of him, the worn denim hugging his muscular thighs. His skin had that warm golden glow that was part sun and part Jack, and his eyes were the color of the ocean in summer. I could feel the waves of heat coming off him. It made me uncomfortable, mostly because I could still feel the attraction between us.

The room was empty except for the two of us. "Where's Kabita? Tommy?"

"Sent them to get dinner."

And they'd listened. Of course. I suppose it made sense. I mean, he was technically my guardian. Or, rather, the guardian of the Key of Atlantis, which was supposedly me. I wasn't sure I bought that entirely, but the facts were sort of stacked against me at the moment.

"And my mother?

"Your mother, I sent home. She looked exhausted."

I felt a flicker of gratitude before I ruthlessly squashed it. Feeling grateful to Jack was a slippery slope to other feelings. Feelings I did not want to examine. "Why are you here?"

His brows rose. "Why wouldn't I be?"

"I mean, how did you know?"

He shook his head. "We're connected, remember?"

"Bullshit. Kabita called you, didn't she?"

He shrugged. "I knew the minute you were in trouble. I just didn't know where you were. When Kabita called, I came as soon as I could. Mostly I just handled...clean up."

Ah. He'd made sure the cops wouldn't stumble upon the kind of crime scene that would have them asking some really uncomfortable questions. The vampire's sweet ride was probably at a chop shop by now. Dammit.

"Find anything interesting?" I asked.

"Actually, yeah." He pulled a smart phone with a lipstick-red cover from inside his beat-up leather jacket and waved it at me. "This was in the car. There's not a lot there, but I did find some notes." A few swipes of his finger over the screen, and he started reading. "'World War Two. Nurse. Swing dancing. Retirement home. Sunny End. Sunny Side. Sunny Park. Doctor...' There's a question mark after that one." He pressed the phone's off button. "That's it. It's odd, though I'm not sure it means anything."

"It might." Things were clicking into place. I pushed the button on the bed control to raise myself up a bit. I ignored the small twinge my head gave at the motion. "She had a soul, Jack. Just like the vamp I killed a few months ago."

He stared at the phone in his hand. "You think she was remembering her past?"

"Sounds like she was remembering something and was keeping track of whatever it was. She mentioned a retirement home. Do you suppose those Sunnys she mentioned are names?"

Jack turned the phone back on. "Sunny End, Sunny Side...yeah, it could be. Why don't I do a bit of research, and then we can check it out together once you're out of here?"

I started to agree, and then stopped as an image of Kabita's reaction swam through my addled brain. I shook my head, ignoring the brief stab of pain that accompanied the movement. "You check them out. Let me know what you find."

A frown marred his almost too-handsome face. "Why? What do you plan on doing?"

"Taking a vacation."

***

I stared, mesmerized, at the Hawaiian dancing doll perched on the dashboard of Tommy's old, beater Chevy pickup. Every time we hit a slight bump in the road, the dancer went from a gentle sway to wild gyrations, the plastic grass of her skirt swooshing madly to and fro. It was about the last thing I'd expected to find in Tommy Wahenaka's truck.

"My granddaughter thought it was funny." He nodded at the hula girl.

I hadn't even known he had a granddaughter. Not that I knew much about him. Tommy played things close to the vest. "When was she in Hawaii?"

"Still there. College."

So Tommy's granddaughter was going to university in Hawaii. Lucky thing. "Oh. Cool." I didn't know what else to say, and Tommy wasn't exactly chatty, so I returned to staring out the window.

We passed a huge wooden sign in a vaguely trapezium shape on the left side of the highway. Brown letters against a pale yellow background announced we were leaving the Mt. Hood National Forest. On the right side of the road was another wooden sign, this one a rectangle with three teepees marching across the middle. Along the top were large letters spelling out "Welcome to Warm Springs." We were officially on reservation land.

The scenery had changed from the lush fir trees and thick undergrowth of the western side of the mountain to the towering pines and stark, naked beauty of the east. We were still at least an hour's drive from Tommy's place.

I decided now was as good a time as any to pick Tommy's brain. "Tommy, have you ever heard of a vampire having a soul?"

I expected him to tell me "no" and leave it at that. Instead, a slight smile curved the shaman's lips. "You're asking the right questions again."

I wasn't sure how to respond, so I kept my mouth shut and my eyes on the road. I figured he'd answer in his own time. That's how Tommy rolled. The pause was so long, I was getting antsy. My head had started throbbing again, and I was seriously thinking about breaking out the hardcore pain meds the doctor had given me.

"You've seen one of them?"

I jerked my focus back, wondering for a moment what on earth he was talking about.

"Yeah, twice now."

"When?" His face remained expressionless, but his voice was grim. His hands tightened on the blue steering wheel. It was the same '70s turquoise color as the body of the truck.

"The first time was a few months ago. Before..." Before all hell broke loose. Before Inigo all but died. "Before we met. The second time was what put me in the hospital."

Tommy appeared to mull it over. "Interesting."

I expected him to say more, but he didn't, so I gave him a little prod. "Trevor says the SRA is experimenting with technology that can put souls into vamps." I knew it was a long shot. Tommy had never worked for the SRA or any other government agency, as far as I knew.

"Not is. Was."

"What?"

The truck barreled down the highway, bursting out of the shade under the pine trees into the bright sunlit flats beyond. Hula girl danced for all she was worth, her plastic smile wide and carefree.

Tommy's gaze was still glued to the road as he swerved into the oncoming lane to pass a slow-moving car. I held my breath as I realized there was a huge semi barreling toward us. Tommy didn't even blink, just moved back into his own lane without missing a beat. I let out a sigh of relief.

"That tech was created nearly thirty years ago," he said finally. "Some idiot scientist figured out a way to take somebody's soul and stuff it into a vampire. Damn fool business."

His answer surprised me. According to Trevor, the tech for soul imbuement was still mostly a pipe dream.

"It was what got your father killed."

My heart was in my throat, fluttering wildly like a trapped bird. I stared at Tommy, eyes wide. I gripped the edge of my seat, my fingers digging into the cheap vinyl. "What?"

Tommy shrugged. "At least in part. Your father threatened to go public. Somebody made sure he didn't."

I wanted to know everything Tommy knew about my father, but he shut his mouth and the door on the subject. All I could do was concentrate on the present. For now.

"You're telling me the Supernatural Regulatory Agency, the very agency I more or less work for, is creating vamps with souls and sending them after me?"

"Not what I said."

I repressed a groan. Tommy was being his usual cryptic self. I shot the old man a glare.

"I saw that." His eyes twinkled, and I swear he was laughing inside.

"Okay, you want to play, I'll play," I said. "If the SRA isn't doing it, someone else is." Hello, Captain Obvious.

Tommy didn't respond. I wasn't surprised. He tended to do that when someone was being unusually thick.

"So, if the SRA isn't using the technology they created, and Trevor is under the impression they're still trying to figure it out, then the likelihood is the technology is no longer in their possession. They're not trying to figure out how to create it, but how to duplicate it."

Tommy nodded.

"But someone out there obviously does have the technology, which means it's highly likely they stole it from the SRA. So the question is: who has the soul vamp technology now? Does the SRA know about them? And how did they steal it in the first place?"

"That's more than one question."

"And yet all the answers are important," I shot back.

That made him smile. "Indeed. The most important question is the one which, when answered, will also answer all the others."

Oh, gods, he was getting all philosophical on me. Still, what he said rang true. "Who has the tech now?"

Tommy pulled onto a side road leading off the main highway. It was frighteningly narrow and riddled with potholes. I knew from my last visit the asphalt would eventually turn into a gravel road, which would then turn into a narrow dirt track before finally petering out in front of Tommy's cabin. As we bounced along, the hula girl gyrated so hard I was sure she'd snap right off the dashboard.

"I can't answer that," Tommy finally said. "Only you know the answer."

I snorted. "If I knew the answer, I wouldn't be asking."

The sigh he heaved spoke volumes about his opinion of my intelligence at the moment. "Who do you know who would be clever enough to steal technology like that, well-connected enough to find a place to use it, and evil enough to send the results gunning for you?"

"Quite frankly, a couple people come to mind." A grim thought struck me. "But only one of them had access to the SRA thirty years ago." My gaze caught Tommy's. My blood ran cold. "Alister Jones has it."

Chapter 13

"Why don't you tell me what's really bothering you." Tommy peered at me over his bowl of venison stew as though daring me to bare my soul.

I swished my spoon through the thick, brown goop. Tommy was inordinately fond of stews, and while they looked tragic, they tasted heavenly. Unfortunately, I wasn't very hungry. The trip had exhausted me. Every bone in my body ached, and the proximity to djinn lands was making the Air power inside me itchy, which in turn was getting the Darkness riled up.

"What do you mean?" When in doubt, play dumb.

Tommy chewed thoughtfully, his eyes never leaving mine. He didn't say a word. Just waited. Awkward.

I let out a sigh. "Well, on top of the soul vamp thing, Brent Darroch escaped from jail. That's not good."

Tommy said nothing. He simply tore a hunk of bread off the homemade artisan loaf in the middle of the table, swiped it through some stew, and popped it in his mouth.

"And, uh, there's that whole price on my head thing. Kind of stressful having vampire bounty hunters on your ass. I'm usually the one hunting them."

Silence. Nothing like a joke that's fallen flat on its face.

"My powers are a little...unpredictable lately," I admitted.

Tommy raised an eyebrow, but said nothing. He was waiting. Waiting for me to say it.

My throat felt thick and tight, and I was half afraid I might do something embarrassing. Like cry. I was clenching my spoon so hard my knuckles turned white. I carefully placed it on the table and forced my muscles to relax. I was only partially successful.

"It's Inigo."

Tommy nodded as though he'd been waiting for me to get to the point. He took another bite of stew and motioned for me to continue.

I wasn't sure how to tell him everything without sharing secrets that weren't mine to tell. "You know his brother, Drago, took him back to dragon lands."

Tommy ripped off another hunk of bread and swirled it through his stew. Still giving me the silent treatment. It was becoming irritating.

"Well, the dragons have a...method for healing. They say they can heal Inigo. Maybe." I tried to swallow past the increasingly large lump in my throat.

"That's good."

"Not really," I said. "Drago said it could take years. Like hundreds of years."

"Ah."

"I'll be dead," I wailed.

"That's a bit dramatic."

Dramatic? Was he mental? I stared at him. Finally I managed to choke out, "You have no idea what I'm going through."

"I'm sure you're right," Tommy said. Was that sarcasm in his tone? Seriously?

"What? So you know what it's like to have the person you love stuck in a century-long coma?" The snark was back.

I could feel the heat rising in my cheeks as he eyed me. "Nope. But I know what it's like to have the person you love die. Lots of people know how that feels. Think you got some kind of monopoly on heartbreak?"

I suddenly felt ashamed. I'd been so busy wallowing in my own misery, I'd been acting like a spoiled little brat. Still, the pain was real, and I was having a hard time dealing with it. At least death was final. This was...something else.

"What's the real problem?" Tommy's tone was softer this time. Sympathetic. It made me want to break down and blubber like a baby.

"The real problem is I don't know what to do. He could wake up tomorrow, or he could wake up never. Or I could be an old woman when he wakes up. I could spend my whole life waiting."

Tommy was quiet so long, I thought he'd gone back to the silent treatment. Finally he said, "Lots of people spend their lives waiting. You wouldn't be the first. You won't be the last. The woman I know you to be would wait forever without batting an eyelash. This is not what upsets you."

"No," I admitted. How did I say this without sounding like a lunatic? "Inigo came to me. In a dream. He told me it would be a very long time before he woke." I stared down at my hands, clenched tightly in my lap. "He told me not to wait."

"Insistently, I gather."

I nodded. "The problem is, I don't know if this was a true dream, or if it was somebody messing with my mind. I don't know what to do." My voice cracked on the last word. I swiped angrily at the hot tears that spilled onto my cheeks.

Tommy leaned back in his chair, the wood squeaking in protest. He steepled his hands across his stomach and stared off into space. "It doesn't matter."

I stared at him. "What?"

"It doesn't matter if the dreams are real or not. It doesn't matter if Inigo wakes up during this millennium or not."

"I don't understand."

Tommy gave me a measured look. "It. Does. Not. Matter." And then he sat there, waiting, as if I would suddenly say something clever.

My mind was an utter blank. Then something sparked, turning my misery to hope. "It doesn't matter because I decide. It's not up to Kabita or Jack or even Inigo. I decide whether I want to wait. Or not." There was just one problem. I didn't think I could make that decision right now. On the one hand, it seemed foolish to put my life on hold, waiting for him to wake up. On the other hand...how could I not wait?

"Don't worry so much," Tommy said, as if reading my mind. "When the time comes to decide, you'll know."

Wonderful. Cryptic Tommy strikes again.

Chapter 14

"This will cost you."

The words were as cold and hard as her perfect face: Morgana, Queen of the Sidhe, perched delicately on a coal-black throne. Her eyes were twin shards of ice as she eyed the man standing before her. She strummed blood-red fingernails on the arms of the throne. "Time travel requires a great deal of power."

Time travel? What the hell?

"Still, it must be done if we are to succeed," the man said, voice firm, unflinching before the Queen.

I couldn't see the speaker's face, but he was tall, well built, with broad shoulders. His distinguished gray hair was neatly trimmed and perfectly styled. Even his dark suit shouted "expensive." We're talking Saville Row expensive.

Every one of my senses screamed at me. I knew this man. But he wouldn't turn around. He wouldn't let me see him.

I figured this was the throne room of Morgana's palace in the Other World, but I couldn't make out much. Everything was fuzzy and indistinct, as though I looked through a fogged windshield. The only things I could see clearly were the queen and the man who stood before her. I was unable to move or shift the perspective. I was an observer, plain and simple.

Morgana sighed. "I suppose you are correct, if we are to set the necessary events in motion." She slowly rose from her throne, the embodiment of fluid grace. Her nearly sheer gown shifted and swirled around her body, revealing a curve here, a hint of shadow there. Strawberry blonde curls fell over her breasts just so, hiding secrets from heated eyes. The queen was a master manipulator, and it was clear her audience of one did not remain unmoved.

"You are ready then, my queen?" There was a thickness to his voice that betrayed arousal. What an idiot. Did he honestly think the Queen of the Sidhe would give him the time of day? I almost felt bad for him. Almost.

"When am I not?" Morgana smiled as she moved toward him, hips swaying seductively. Her lush lips parted to reveal that tiny gap between her front teeth.

It was not a question, and her visitor did not provide an answer. Instead, he held out his arm in a gentlemanly fashion. The familiarity of the gesture sent shivers down my spine. Yes, I definitely knew him. I just couldn't place him.

The queen took his arm with her right hand. With her left, she gave a languid wave. The air in front of them began to shimmer as a circle formed from nothing. It grew more solid until it was a rippling silver disc suspended in midair. Then the two of them stepped through and disappeared.

"What the hell?" I spoke aloud, or thought I did, but no sound came out. I tried to move toward the disc, but my feet were anchored in place. Right, I was just an observer.

I was about to issue a few choice albeit silent cuss words when suddenly the world tipped and tilted so fast, I thought I might tumble off. When it righted itself, I was no longer in the throne room. Instead I was in a darkened bedroom, an ordinary place where two girls slept peacefully.

A shimmering disc formed next to the bed, and two dark forms stepped through: the queen and her visitor. Dread lodged in my stomach.

Letting go of her escort's arm, the queen leaned over the bed. She glanced from one girl to the next before choosing the one with the light-colored hair. Placing her hands on either side of the girl's face, the queen closed her eyes. I could feel Morgana as she began to draw power from the Other Side. A lot of power. She was about to do something big.

My jaw dropped as she sank her fingers through the girl's skull and into her brain. I tried to say something, but nothing came out. Again, I was rooted to the floor in silence, a mere observer to the horror.

Morgana swirled her fingers around in the sleeping girl's brain like she was stirring a pot of soup. The girl moved uneasily and let out a little moan of pain. Slowly Morgana withdrew her fingers. As she did, she pulled out a tiny, shimmering gold thread from the sleeping girl's brain. At least, that's what it looked like.

Morgana handed the thread to the man whose face I still couldn't make out. "These are the memories you wish to erase."

The man stared at the delicate thread cupped in his palm. Then he closed his fist around it and crushed it. It fell from his fingers in a trickle of blackened dust.

Morgana gave the man a wry smile. "I shall replace them with that which we discussed."

The man said nothing, simply nodded. Once again, Morgana reached into the girl's head, stirring her fingers slowly. This time when she pulled them out, no threads came with them, but her fingers shimmered silver in the moonlight.

"It is done."

The man offered Morgana his arm again and they exited the way they'd come, through the disc, clearly a portal between the human world and the Other World. It closed behind them, leaving me standing in the girls' bedroom.

As if their passing had broken some kind of spell, I was suddenly able to move. I hurried to the bed, squatting down to get a good look at the blond girl's face. What I saw made me gasp.

***

I woke to sunlight streaming through the window. It was much brighter than I was used to. Portland mornings were often on the gray and gloomy side this time of year. Central Oregon mornings were a whole different animal. With a grunt, I pulled the blankets over my head to block out the light. Didn't Tommy believe in curtains?

The rich scent of coffee tickled my nose. I could hear Tommy banging around in the kitchen. A glance at my cellphone told me it was way too freaking early in the morning, but there was no way I was getting back to sleep.

Last night's conversation was still fresh in my mind, but I wasn't quite ready to face it yet. Tommy had said I'd know when I was ready. Today was not that day. Instead, I replayed my dream. Yeah, Cordy told me I couldn't always trust them, but this had all the hallmarks of one of my Atlantean-influenced dreams.

I fingered the amulet around my neck. Yes, this had definitely been a true dream. A dream of the past. That was why I couldn't change anything; it had already happened.

I sat up abruptly, ignoring the slight dizziness as my body tried to deal with the whole being awake thing. The blonde girl from my dream had been Jade Vincent. Much younger, much more innocent, and a hell of a lot happier, but definitely Jade.

Morgana had taken memories from her. Of what, I had no idea, but I imagined they must be good ones, happy ones. The kind of memories that gave a person solid ground under her feet. Morgana had replaced those memories with what? The only reason the Fairy Queen would expend that kind of power on a nobody girl was so she could use it to her advantage. Whatever memories she'd implanted in Jade's mind had been used to manipulate the poor girl. Who she was, what she'd done, was based on a lie.

Rage infused me. Morgana and her sidekick or partner or whoever had traveled back in time and turned an innocent girl into a psychotic killer. Of that I had no doubt. And now I knew who I'd seen in the Other World with the Fairy Queen.

Alister Jones. I was sure of it. Who else could it be?

I slipped from bed, jaw clenched so hard I thought my teeth might crack. That bastard had a lot to answer for. Clearly, he was in cahoots with Morgana. Obviously, he must need her help for his plans for world domination. Though what he could possibly offer her was beyond me.

And why was Jade so damned important? I'd felt the kind of power Morgana had used to get them through the portal into the past and fix Jade's memories. It was a lot, even for the Fairy Queen. Why? Why would she do all this? What did she have to gain?

Morgana was definitely up to something that went far beyond her tiff with me and her hatred of the djinn.

I shook my head. It was way too early for any sort of logical thinking. Not that logic was much use where Morgana was involved. What I needed now was a very large cup of Tommy's coffee.

I threw on a pair of sweats and headed down the hall toward the kitchen. If Tommy was going to make coffee for me every morning, I might just move in permanently.

Chapter 15

"Again." Tommy thumped his walking stick on the ground.

"Seriously?" My whole body ached and my brain felt like it was stuffed with cotton. "You're killing me. This is cruel and unusual punishment. I'm pretty sure there's a law against that."

His weathered face remained impassive, but his eyes narrowed. "Again."

I'd been at Tommy's for almost a week, and every single day we'd done the same thing: practice. And not just physical stuff, though there'd been plenty of that. Tommy claimed it was his version of physical therapy. The real practice, though, was the power drills. As in my very special, super-duper Atlantean powers. Since Air was the newest power, we worked on that the most. It was exhausting.

"I can't, Tommy. I'm tired." I winced at the slight whine in my voice. I was no sissy, but I was reaching the end of my rope. My powers had a mind of their own.

"You're tired because you fight against yourself," Tommy snapped. "You are tired because you allow your emotions to affect your powers, and right now your emotions are out of control. Stop wallowing in self-pity and control will follow. Now, again."

Clearly I'd get no sympathy from Tommy. I sighed, glancing around the flat plain of sage brush, rock, and a few spring grasses struggling to survive. Nope. Nobody to save me from the torture. I closed my eyes to focus on summoning the air again.

"Open."

My eyes flew open. "What?"

He shook his head at me like I was some kind of idiot. "You gonna close your eyes in the middle of a fight?" he asked, thumping his stick again. "Or when a demon's charging at you? I don't think so. Again. Eyes open."

What I really wanted to do was throw something at him. Preferably something sharp and pointy. Instead, I did what he told me.

It was a struggle, focusing on the powers inside me without closing my eyes. The Darkness and Fire were right there, eager to get out and play. They'd been frighteningly easy to work with, or at least they'd been easy to let out. Not so easy to rein in. But it was the Air I wanted. Typically, it was doing its own thing, unconcerned with cooperation. Tommy said it was my emotions causing the problem, but it seemed par for the course to me.

In my mind's eye, Air appeared as tendrils of silvery mist whirling and twirling their way around that deep, dark, inner well where my powers lived. I tried to coax it, but it ignored me.

"Don't ask it," Tommy snapped. "Tell it. You're the boss." He pointed a gnarled finger at me for emphasis.

"Right. Sure," I muttered under my breath. "I'm the boss."

"I heard that."

I ignored him and focused on the Air again. "Whirlwind."

It ignored me.

"Whirlwind." I gave it a little more force.

Nothing.

"Damn you," I snapped. "Give me a bloody whirlwind."

This time, something happened. It just wasn't the something I expected.

Green light shot from the center of my chest and out the tips of my fingers. I stared at my hands as if they belonged to an alien. "What the..."

The ground beneath my feet heaved violently, tossing me onto my butt like I was a rag doll. Holy crap. Was that an earthquake?

I reached out to brace myself, and where my hands touched dirt, weeds and grasses sprang up. They grew wild and green and huge, far bigger than they should have in the dry ground of the high desert. They grew until I was surrounded by a thicket and Tommy was blocked from view.

Panic surged through me as the green light intensified. I yanked my hands from the dirt, but it was too late. Trees joined the grasses, erupting from the ground, changing from tiny saplings into towering evergreens within moments. Vines twisted and twined around tree trunks and branches. Orchids sprouted from the bark. Orchids. In Central Oregon.

I scrambled to my feet, trying to push my way through the thicket back to Tommy. It was no use. Everywhere I touched, something new and green sprang up until I was completed fenced in by a thick wall of flora.

Tommy thumped his stick again, and this time I felt the vibration through the earth. Slowly, the green light that surrounded me retreated, sinking back inside me. It mumbled things in a language I couldn't even begin to comprehend, but the tone was sullen. I stood there with my mouth hanging open, my brain a frozen blank.

A pair of gnarled brown hands poked through the weeds and branches, parting them like curtains. Tommy appeared, dark eyes sparkling with merriment. "Now, that's what I'm talking about."

***

"What the hell was that?" I dusted dirt and debris off my butt. "Was there an earthquake or something?" I pushed my way through the thick greenery, purposefully ignoring the fact that it hadn't been there a minute ago. I did not want to go there.

Tommy's dark eyes danced in amusement, the lines bracketing his mouth deepening ever so slightly. He propped both hands on his walking stick as he eyed me. "Earthquake? Yes."

"Didn't think you got many earthquakes this side of the mountain." I know. I know. Denial, thy name is Morgan. And yet, it wasn't that I was in denial exactly. More that I already had so much to deal with, I was afraid one more Atlantean superpower might send me over the edge.

"We don't." He just leaned on his damn stick and smiled at me.

I huffed out a breath. "Fine. It was me, okay? I did it. That green stuff. What the hell is going on?"

He eyeballed me. "Do you remember what I asked you about your powers the day we met?"

I mulled it over a moment, remembering. It had been here at his cabin. I'd been in search of djinn lands, hunting a killer. "Yeah, you asked how many powers were inside me."

"And what was your answer?"

"Three. You told me there would be six..." Oh, holy crap. If he was right, I had four now. Earth power had joined the others. Two more to go.

He must have seen reality slap me across the face, because he gave me an approving nod. "The ancients called it being kissed by moonlight."

"Moonlight? Why?"

"You ask a lot of questions," he said. "Now, let's try it again."

Oh, gods. "You want me to cause an earthquake?"

"Well, I'm not asking you to dance the limbo."

I snorted with laughter. Oh, he was a snarky one. "What if I make another one of those?" I jerked my thumb at the mini jungle.

Tommy shrugged. "Then I have some nice landscaping."

I guessed I wasn't getting out of it. I moved a few feet away from him and carefully braced myself, feet apart, knees slightly bent. Closing my eyes, I tried to focus on what was inside me.

"Eyes open."

"Excuse me?" I shot Tommy a glare. "How am I supposed to focus on this new power with my eyes open?" It was one thing to call Fire or Darkness that way. I was more or less used to them by now, and they came when I called. I just didn't like calling them. They had a tendency to take over and that could get really ugly. Anything new required massive amounts of concentration.

"Like I said before, you gonna stop in the middle of a fight to focus? Vamps don't care if you got a new power. They just want to rip your throat out."

I gave him an aggravated look, but kept my eyes open as I reached down toward my powers. The usual suspects jumped to eager attention, but I ignored them. I only wanted one, my new superpower: Earth.

It lurked in the corners, a faint green mist. I could tell it wanted to come out and play, but only on its own terms and in its own time. It didn't want me in control. Well, tough.

I wasn't sure how this new power worked, so I visualized it swirling around me and shooting out my fingertips like it had before. I swear, it gave me the mental finger before it gave in and did what I wanted.

Unlike the other powers, which had a tendency to surge up and out of me fast and hard, Earth simply oozed out of my pores. My vision misted over, like I was looking through green-tinted glass, and I could see the shimmer of green power dancing and curling over my skin like vines twining around a tree trunk.

I gave the green power a vision of an earthquake. Before I'd even finished the thought, green light shot from my fingertips again and the ground gave a violent heave. It buckled and roiled, throwing me to the ground with enough force to knock the wind out of me. The earth fissured, cracks racing out across the high desert as wave after wave of violence rocked the surface.

"Enough!"

Tommy stood over me, his expression fierce. Even the green paid attention. Its reaction was the sulking of a chastised child. The ground stopped shaking and cracking. The light stopped shooting out of my fingers and the shimmer of green sank back into my skin. My vision returned to normal. The metaphorical lid I kept on my powers slammed shut with an insolent clang.

"Holy crap." Okay, not one of my more intelligent responses, but it was the only thing that came to mind as I lay there on my back in the high desert grasses staring up at Tommy. Sagebrush poked me in the butt. It wasn't terribly comfortable.

"Indeed. Once more. Only this time, I want you to focus your power on that rock."

I squinted in the direction he was jabbing his stick. It was a decent-sized boulder, but it had to be a good quarter-mile away or more. No way I had that kind of focus. Not yet. "You have got to be kidding."

"Not even remotely."

I sighed as I clambered to my feet again. I was tired, I ached all over, and I was pretty sure there was a giant bruise on my butt. Earthquaking a rock to death was the last thing I wanted to do. The only thing I was interested in doing was taking a nice long soak in Tommy's ancient metal bathtub while drowning my sorrows with whatever gods-awful tea he had stashed around the cabin. I could really use something stronger, but unfortunately for me, Tommy didn't drink alcohol.

"Focus," Tommy snapped, thumping his walking stick. I swear I wanted to grab that stick and whack him with it. He smirked as if he'd heard my thoughts. "Try it."

"Fine," I snapped. "Focusing."

Planting my feet firmly on the ground again, I visualized the powers inside me, coaxing up the greenish mist that was Earth power. As it sifted through my pores once again, the ground shifted slightly beneath my feet.

"Just the rock," Tommy admonished.

Before I could sass him back, the sound of a car horn interrupted my focus. The green misty stuff sank back under my skin and curled up into a petulant ball. It clearly had no plans for any further cooperation. Saved by the bell.

***

Jack was driving a brand new, shiny red pickup truck that looked totally out of place parked next to Tommy's rustic cabin and old blue Chevy. Sure, trucks were a dime a dozen here on the eastern side of the mountain, but they tended to be coated in dust, rust, and other unpleasant things. Shiny, they were not.

He strode toward Tommy and me, all long legs and lean muscles and flowing, sun-streaked hair. My heart gave an unexpected and unwanted flutter. I'd loved him once. Maybe a part of me still did. I just wasn't sure my heart could handle what he'd do to it. Besides, I still hadn't decided anything about Inigo. I gave my heart a stern mental talking to.

"You're a day early," I said as he drew closer. I'd asked him to pick me up in a week.

"I know," he said, nodding to Tommy in greeting. "But I've got a lead on that vampire that attacked you. Thought you might want to come along for the ride. If you're up to it?"

Up to it? I'd been healed for days, and I'd do just about anything to get away from Tommy's ceaseless drills. "Sure. Sounds good. I'll just grab my stuff."

As I took off for the cabin at a jog, I could feel Tommy's eyes boring into me like twin lasers. I knew without a doubt this little training session of ours wouldn't be our last, and that was probably a good thing. Much as I hated them, Tommy's drills had helped me focus. They'd helped me heal. And not just physically.

I wouldn't miss his rock-hard guest bed, though. I grinned as I dumped my suitcase on top of the mattress and started tossing my stuff into it. I hadn't come with much, so I was done and out the door in minutes.

Before I hopped into the truck, I gave Tommy a quick hug. He smelled of sage and juniper and wood smoke. "Thanks for the training. Sorry I have to leave early." I wasn't sorry.

"Liar. Don't worry about it. You'll be back." His eyes promised all sorts of revenge.

"I don't doubt it." I turned to climb up into the pickup, but Tommy's hand on my arm stopped me.

"Remember, there will come a day, very soon, when you will have to make a choice." His eyes were deadly serious. "When that time comes, you must choose wisely. Your choice...it could alter the future."

"Okay." I had to make choices every day. Life-or-death kinds of choices. I couldn't understand what he was trying to tell me. He was definitely a little over the top. Alter the entire future? I doubted it. "I'll, uh, do my best."

"Just remember, choose with the heart of a woman, not a warrior. It will not lead you astray."

He let me go then. Baffled, I climbed into the truck, slamming the door shut. As we bounced down the road in a cloud of dust, I craned my head to look out the back window. Tommy was still standing in the middle of the road. I watched him until we turned the corner, and Tommy and the cabin disappeared from sight.

Chapter 16

The wooden sign next to the street proudly proclaimed "Sunnyside Village," complete with curlicues and fake gold paint that was starting to flake off. Beneath the name, neat black letters proclaimed it to be "An award winning community of elegance and style for the retired."

In other words? Old folks' home. And it looked like one, too. Screw "retirement village," this place looked more like a prison. Okay, maybe not a prison, but I wasn't seeing a whole lot of elegance or style. Unless "depressing" was a style.

The building looked like it might have once been a single family ranch-style house. It was long and low with '60s era aluminum framed windows and worn vinyl siding painted a dull gray. At some point, somebody had added a couple extra wings to house the retirees and decided to paint them beige. No doubt beige paint had been on sale. It didn't help with the elegance.

Its saving grace was that Sunnyside Village was perched on the side of a hill overlooking Happy Valley and Sunnyside Road in the hills just outside Portland. It wasn't a bad view. At least the inmates—I mean guests—didn't have to look at the building. Talk about depressing.

It was weird, too, because Happy Valley was known as a sort of posh place where people lived in huge cookie-cutter houses and drove gas-guzzling SUVs that took up three whole parking spaces. They shopped at snazzy grocery stores that had wide, brightly lit aisles and sold organic food for insane prices. Most everything was new and clean and fresh.

Not Sunnyside Village. It stuck out like a proverbial sore thumb; a dandelion among peonies.

Jack led the way inside with me tromping along behind him. The place was giving me the willies, and I wasn't in the mood to hide it. My booted feet *thunk*ed angrily on the concrete steps leading up to the front doors.

"Chill," Jack hissed at me.

A nine-hundred-year-old warrior and former Templar knight telling me to chill? That made me giggle. But I took his suggestion onboard and stopped the tromping. Instead, I gave my purple corduroy jacket a tug and smoothed down my black skirt. That's right: skirt. I'd swapped my usual leather jacket and jeans for something more professional. I refused to give up the boots, though. A girl's got to have standards.

We passed through the glass double doors and into the interior of the building. The original living room had been turned into a front office, the carpet replaced with ugly vinyl tiles in white and gray, the kind you find in public bathrooms the world over. The walls were painted the same dull gray as the outside, and the counter that had been added was made of cheap pine and gray-speckled white Formica. They must have salvaged that from the kitchen or something.

The only spot of color and interest was the original brick fireplace. The opening had been boarded up, but the rest had been left as is. Somebody had placed a vase of pink and blue silk flowers on the mantle, no doubt thinking it would brighten up the place. Unfortunately, they just looked cheap and tacky.

Above the mantle hung a picture in a garish, gold frame. A pudgy man stared down upon us through thick-lensed glasses, a benevolent smile on his lips. A small brass plaque on the bottom of the frame no doubt identified the man, but I didn't need to read it to guess this was the facility's medical director, the man we'd come to see.

The woman behind the front desk was plainly bored out of her skull. In fact, I'd bet just about anything that, despite her appearance of business-like efficiency, she was actually playing Tetris. Couldn't say I blamed her.

Jack cleared his throat. She ignored him. Sort of. I could see her giving him the once-over out of the corner of her eye. Couldn't blame her for that, either. He'd also dressed for the occasion in a dark suit that emphasized his narrow waist and broad shoulders, and a blue button-down shirt that brought out the color of his eyes. He was, admittedly, extremely tasty in that get up.

"Excuse me, Miss," he said.

Miss? Despite the bleached-blond hair and frosted pink lipstick, the woman wasn't a day under sixty. The red plastic nametag pinned to her ample chest read "Doris."

"How may I help you?" Doris finally glanced up from her computer screen, carefully patting her hair into place with a pudgy hand and adjusting the hot pink sweater draped over her shoulders. If the expression in her eyes was anything to go by, Jack was in serious danger of losing his suit.

"Dr. Jackson Keel. This is my assistant, Ms. Bailey. We have an appointment with Dr. Mickleson."

"Oh, yes, you called yesterday."

I swear to the gods, she fluttered her eyelashes at Jack.

"Let me show you to Dr. Mickleson's office." Doris started to get up, but Jack waved her back down.

"Thank you, Doris,"—he put just the right purr into her name—"but I don't want to take up your valuable time. Just point the way." He gave her a smile oozing with sex appeal. I barely refrained from making a gagging motion.

Doris beamed at him. "Down the hall, third door on the left. Can I get you anything? Tea? Coffee?"

"No, thank you. Doris." Jack gave her another one of his blinding smiles that sent the poor woman's ample bosom heaving. She actually picked up a patient chart and started fanning herself with it.

I managed to repress my smirk long enough to make our way past the front desk and down the hall. "She wanted to eat you alive." I couldn't help a small giggle.

Jack scowled. "Shut up."

That made me laugh even harder.

We were in part of the original building. Bedrooms had been turned into offices, no doubt. The third door on the left had a strip of red plastic that matched Doris's name tag. The white letters proclaimed this was the office of Dr. M. Mickleson. Jack gave a quick rap and entered at the muffled response from inside. I trailed behind him, pulling a small notebook out of my pocket, playing the part of the dutiful assistant.

The first thing I noticed was the smell of aftershave; the office reeked of it. Something sharp and musky. It made my nose itch. I managed to repress a sneeze at the cost of making my eyes water.

The man behind the desk matched the woman at the front: short and slightly pudgy. They even had matching name tags and expressions of boredom. He did not, however, sport a hot pink sweater. His was navy. His hair was more salt than pepper with a shiny bald spot on top. I recognized him from the photo above the fireplace.

The men shook hands in that macho way they do. Mickleson ignored me, focusing his attention on Jack through thick glasses with chunky black plastic frames. I wasn't used to men ignoring me. Thanks to my more than generous curves and bright red hair I sort of stood out, but it was clear Mickleson was more interested in Jack's supposed status. As a mere assistant, I was beneath his notice.

"Ah, Dr. Keel. So nice of you to pay us a visit." Mickelson's tone didn't sound like he thought it was nice. More like he thought it was an imposition. His watery hazel eyes narrowed suspiciously. "Please sit." He waved us to a pair of plain wooden chairs that were insanely uncomfortable. Probably another thing they'd salvaged from the kitchen. "I understand you have a question about one of our former patients?"

"Possibly, Dr. Mickleson." Jack leaned forward as if about to impart a deep, dark secret. "You see, doctor, we have a most interesting conundrum, and since you are an expert in the field, we hope you can help us."

Dr. Mickleson steepled his fingers together, excitement flitting briefly across his face before he managed to school his expression. His eyes sparkled behind the thick lenses of his glasses, suspicion suddenly erased. He was on the hook. "I would be glad to help in any way I can. What seems to be the problem?"

"As you know, my practice is in geriatric psychology. Experimental, of course."

I almost sputtered over that, but Mickleson nodded eagerly. I guess there really was such a thing. Or he wanted there to be.

"Of course, Dr. Keel. Go on."

"Recently, a patient was brought to me suffering from dementia. She was found wandering the streets, confused. She remembers almost nothing of her past. I am trying to track where she came from so I can access her files and hopefully help her."

I heard the odd emphasis on "help" and knew what Mickleson was no doubt thinking. "Experiment on" was probably close, and Mickleson seemed way too eager to assist us. It made me wonder just what kinds of things were going on behind closed doors here.

"Of course. Of course. If you could give me some details..." Mickleson leaned forward, licking his thick lips.

"She remembers being a nurse in the Second World War, dancing to big band music, and living in a retirement home that includes the name 'Sunny.' That's it, I'm afraid," Jack said, leaning back in his chair. His tone was casual, but he watched Mickleson like a hawk.

During Jack's description, Mickleson's face had slowly drained of color. His mouth opened and closed a few times, and finally he squeaked out, "But she's..."

I knew what he'd been about to say: dead. Instead, he shook his head, sweat popping out along his upper lip and his eyes going wide with panic. He stood up quickly, flapping his pudgy hands to indicate we should do the same.

"I'm sorry, Dr. Keel, but I'm afraid we have no such patient here, nor have we ever. I'm so sorry you wasted your time." He herded us toward the door. "I really wish I could help you."

"As do I," Jack murmured. "She must have come from another facility. We have several more on our list to check."

"Yes, yes. I'm sure that's it. Well, have a nice day." Mickelson all but slammed the door in our faces.

I waited until we were back outside. "He's just about the best liar ever." My voice dripped with sarcasm.

Jack snorted. "No kidding."

"Now what?" Mickleson wasn't going to spill his guts without a little persuasion.

"Now," Jack said, climbing into my car, "we wait."

Chapter 17

We didn't have long to wait. Less than an hour later, Mickelson appeared at the side door of the Sunnyside Village main building. After a furtive glance around, he quickly crossed the small parking lot and hopped into a brand new Chevy Camaro in bumblebee yellow. The car roared to life, and Mickleson took off in the direction of the freeway.

"Total penis car," I muttered.

Jack snorted with laughter. "At least he'll be easy to follow."

"You got that right."

I pulled into traffic, keeping a couple of vehicles between my Mustang and Mickelson's shiny yellow car as we drove north on I205, then west on I84 into downtown Portland. Twenty minutes later, he pulled up in front of a small restaurant tucked in between a couple of larger brick buildings, completely ignoring the fact he was blocking a fire hydrant. As he disappeared through the turquoise door, I pulled into a loading zone across the street. Through the large front window, Jack and I had a clear view into the busy restaurant.

The doctor rushed through the dining room, giving a brief wave to the wait staff, who seemed to barely notice his presence. He slipped through a swinging door in the back, which no doubt led to the kitchen, vanishing from sight. Wherever he was going, he seemed in an all-fire hurry to get there.

I moved to get out of the car, but Jack grabbed my arm. "Not yet."

I shot him a scowl. "No way am I letting him slip away without finding out what's up."

"And what if he comes back and catches you? We'll find out more if we wait. Trust me."

Gods, I was sick to death of waiting, but I settled back into my seat and kept my eyes glued to the restaurant. I desperately wanted to know what was going on in there.

Five minutes ticked by with all the speed of five hours. Then ten. Fifteen. Finally, Dr. Mickleson emerged from the restaurant looking flushed and worried. He swiped a blue handkerchief across his face, then jumped into his bumblebee car and took off back toward the freeway.

"Okay, now." Jack nodded toward the restaurant.

I hopped out of the car and strode casually across the street. The inside of the restaurant was just as chaotic and noisy as it had looked from the outside. A harried waiter shook his head as he approached me, a tray full of steaming hot noodles on one arm. "Sorry, but we're full. If you want to wait..."

"I'm here to meet someone."

He frowned. "Uh, okay. Name?"

"Dr. Mickleson."

The waiter shook his head as he peered at the reservations list. "Nothing here under that name."

"Short, grayish hair with a bald spot, black hipster glasses..."

"Oh, yeah. Sorry, lady, you just missed him," the waiter interrupted. "He left less than five minutes ago." He started toward one of the tables with his tray of food.

"Really?" I gave him my best baffled expression, stepping into his path. "But he said to meet him here at one o'clock. I'm a little early. He left already? We haven't even eaten."

"I don't know what he told you, but he wasn't here to eat." The waiter moved around me to deposit the noodle bowls in front of customers at the table. Empty tray in hand, he turned and sped off toward the kitchen.

"Wait." I hurried after him. "What do you mean? Why did he leave?"

"Listen, lady, I'm busy, okay?"

"Please." I gave him my best innocent expression and a twenty dollar bill. "I could really use your help."

He sighed, snagging the twenty before retying the strings of his black apron. "Fine. All I know is that dude rents out the basement from the landlord. We let him through whenever he wants access. No questions. That's where he went today. Then he left."

"But we were supposed to have a meeting. It's important." I doubted the young man was going to tell Mickelson or anyone else that I'd been here, but I kept up the charade, just in case.

"He didn't make a reservation, and he didn't say anything about meeting anyone." The waiter shot me an exasperated look as he stuffed the twenty into his back pocket. "Please lady, I got shit to do. Why don't you call his cellphone or something?" He wheeled toward the kitchen, grumbling under his breath.

"Thanks," I said, but the door had already swung shut behind him. I couldn't help grinning as I exited the restaurant and slid into the car.

"Why do you look like the cat that ate the canary?" Jack asked.

"Because I just found out something very interesting about Mickleson." I shared what I'd learned. "I've no idea why on earth he'd be renting a basement, let alone one so far away from his office, or why he would come here straight after meeting with us. But it's got to mean something, right?"

"Interesting." Jack eyed the restaurant entrance. "Very interesting."

There was something in his tone. "You know something. Spill."

"That particular restaurant sits above the Shanghai Tunnels. It's not the main entrance the tours use, but it's one of the few buildings that still has direct access to the tunnels."

The Shanghai Tunnels were a series of underground passages that had once connected just about every basement of every building in old downtown Portland. Mostly they'd been used for delivery of goods to various shops, but some said they'd been used to deliver a lot more than that. Legend had it, they'd been used to shanghai men to crew the ships waiting in port. Hence the name.

"Well, he couldn't be doing anything too nefarious, then," I said. "They do tours down there all the time."

"Not everywhere," Jack said. "There are still plenty of tunnels and rooms that have been blocked off by cave-ins or bricked up by the owners. Just because he's renting the basement of this restaurant doesn't mean that's where he's actually doing... whatever it is he's doing."

Good point. I watched the busy restaurant. A group of young twenty-somethings in business attire exited the restaurant, laughing and chatting. A couple of them carried little white boxes of leftovers. "We can't exactly waltz in there now. Too many people."

"Agreed. We'll come back tonight after they've closed."

"You don't think it'll be too late? That Mickleson will have gotten rid of...whatever by then?"

Jack shook his head. "He has no idea we're onto him. He thinks we're just trying to find information on some lost old lady."

"We're onto him? Really? Because I don't know about you, but I have no idea what the hell he's up to."

"Smart ass."

That made me laugh.

***

I was sort of glad any further investigations had been put on hold. I may have been fully healed, more or less, but I was exhausted. I wasn't sure if it was from the healing itself, or Tommy's version of physical therapy.

At least my new superpower hadn't put in any more appearances. It seemed content to mellow out with the rest of the gang, and that was fine with me.

I let myself into my house and kicked off my boots. Leaving them at the door, I padded in stocking feet down the hall to my bedroom and fell face-first on the bed.

I don't even remember falling asleep.

I lay spread-eagle on a hard surface. Not smooth. Small stones and bits of what felt like roots or branches poked painfully into my back. Overhead, tree limbs covered thickly in rich green leaves nearly blocked out the sun, turning the area around me into a verdant twilight.

I tried to sit up, but my legs and arms wouldn't move. I turned my head and stared at my right wrist, realizing it was trapped beneath a thick twist of vine and root. Same went for my other wrist and, I imagined, both ankles, since they were immobilized, too.

"What the hell?" I struggled against my bindings, but they only drew tighter the harder I fought.

"I suggest you do not resist, Dara." The female voice was light and musical, but underneath lurked something dark and dangerous.

"How do you know my name? What do you want? Who are you? Why are you doing this?" I cast about, trying to catch a glimpse of my captor, but she stood well out of the line of sight.

"So many questions." Her tone was taunting. "I know many things about you, Dara Boyd."

"Listen, bitch," I snarled, showing her my tough side, the one that kept me safe and everyone else at bay. "You better let me up, or else..."

"Or else what?" This time there was no lightness, only the threat of danger.

"Listen, lady, I've got friends." It was a lie. I had no friends. Nobody cared about me. No one would notice if I was gone. Not even my girlfriend, though she might miss my half of the rent money.

"They will hunt you down and kick your ass. You don't want to do anything you'll regret."

Suddenly, my captor's face came into view, inches above mine. She was breathtakingly beautiful. So beautiful, it made my heart ache. Her hair was the color of a sunset and her pale skin glowed like the moon. Her breasts swelled under her shimmering gown, a hint of cleavage revealed by the plunging neckline. Between her parted lips, I saw a tiny gap in her teeth. It was oddly endearing and sexy as hell.

But then I looked in her eyes, and what I saw there was anything but endearing. Wells of blackness swirled there. A darkness so unending, it filled me with horror.

"Regret?" she whispered, her breath warm against my face. "You have no idea what that word means. But you will."

She placed her hand on the center of my chest. For a moment I felt nothing. Then I felt a pain beyond anything I'd ever dreamed of.

I screamed.

***

I sat bolt upright in bed, pillow clutched to my chest. My heart was pounding so hard I thought it might just crack a rib. Remnants of pain drifted away, along with the fog in my brain.

I yanked the neck of my tank top away from my chest, half-expecting to see the imprint of a hand there. Nothing. My skin was smooth, unblemished. No burn mark. No blisters.

I heaved a sigh of relief, rubbing my breast bone. Gods, these dreams had to stop. I had a bad feeling that one day, they'd go too far, and I'd end up getting hurt for real.

Sliding to the edge of the mattress, I dangled my feet over the side. I gave my neck a careful stretch, noting the muscles were tense and sore.

The dream wasn't hard to figure out. I knew exactly who I'd been in this dream: Dara Boyd, aka Jade Vincent, dragon hunter and psycho bitch extraordinaire. Though if my dreams were anything to go on, there was a very good reason why she was batshit crazy.

Because I'd also known the other woman in my dream, the woman who'd trapped and tortured the very young teenage girl who had once been Dara Boyd. Who'd stolen her memories and planted gods knew what in their place. The same woman who'd caught me in her web of revenge: Morgana, Queen of the Sidhe.

Chapter 18

There was just enough time before I met Jack to stop by my friend Cordelia's place of business. I was feeling a desperate need to see her face to face, not just as a voice on the line. Cordelia read tarot, palms, and crystal balls down at Fringe, a nightclub for Portland's more paranormal residents. Cordy was the real deal, too, not some charlatan trying to make a fast buck. She had actual contacts on the other side.

It was early in the evening, so Fringe was pretty empty. I gave the bartender a wave as I passed through. He nodded, indicating Cordelia was free. I still hadn't figured out exactly what kind of supernatural species he was. More than human, that was for sure. While he was friendly, he was always cautious around me, never letting anything slip, which made me even more curious.

Cordelia's spot was in an alcove off the dance floor. A shimmering silver curtain gave the illusion of privacy and a sense of drama. I pushed my way through into the inner sanctum and had to bite my lower lip to keep from laughing.

Cordy was decked out in a flowing robe of dark blue silk trimmed in gold fringe. There was an antebellum mansion in Georgia that wanted its curtains back. On her head was a purple and gold turban sprouting peacock feathers, and she wore more makeup than an '80s hair band.

"Oh, go ahead. Laugh."

A small giggle escaped. "Sorry, you just look..."

"More ridiculous than usual?" Cordy rolled her eyes and tucked a stray strand of dark hair up under her turban. "Tell me about it. The boss thinks it adds drama or something. He believes the clients will like it. Unfortunately for me, they do."

"The boss" was Fringe's mysterious owner. He was a supernatural of some kind, but, like the bartender, I had no idea what kind. I'd never seen more of him than a vague shadow. He was scary as hell, and he made sure to keep everyone in his club on the straight and narrow. Fringe had a zero tolerance policy when it came to violence, which was a good thing with all the random species running around. Some of them were not very fond of each other.

"How can I help?" Cordelia asked, waving me into the seat opposite her, the rings on her fingers sparkling in the candlelight.

I plopped into a chair on the other side of the little round table holding Cordelia's crystal ball. "I had another dream."

She gazed at me, blue eyes serious. "Okay. Who were you this time?"

It was a legitimate question. In my dreams I'd been everything from an ancient Atlantean priest to a woman jumping off a cliff. It was enough to give a girl a complex.

"Remember that psycho dragon hunter we took down a few months ago? The one that tried to murder...Inigo." My throat tightened so I could barely squeeze out his name. The ache in my chest was a vicious throb.

"Jade?" A frown marred Cordelia's otherwise smooth forehead. "You're dreaming her memories? Why?"

"I was hoping you could answer that."

"What aren't you telling me?" Her voice was stern.

Cordelia Nightwing was nothing if not perceptive. "There was someone else in my dreams." I lowered my voice. No way I wanted anyone overhearing this. "The Queen of the Sidhe. In the dream, she was torturing me. I mean Jade. She was also in cahoots with Alister Jones. She stole some of Jade's memories at his behest and replaced them with something else. I don't know what."

"Oh, my." Cordelia's eyes widened. "Why? What did they want?"

"Beats me," I said with a shrug. "The dream never went that far."

Cordy pulled a silk folding fan from somewhere within her voluminous robe and began fanning herself vigorously. "Cripes."

"I know, right?"

She mulled things over for a minute, tapping one long black-lacquered nail on the red silk table cloth while continuing to waft her fan around. Her eyes took on a faraway look. "I have a feeling this is all tied into whatever you're investigating right now. Tell me about it."

I gave her a quick run-down on the soul vampires, Darroch's escape from Area 51, and how Alister was probably behind it all. I left out the bit about my dad. That was personal, and it wasn't part of the investigation, exactly. "What I don't understand is how the Fairy Queen is involved in all of that. If she is."

"Oh, she is. I've no doubt of that." Cordelia said.

I almost asked her how she knew, and then realized what a stupid question that would be. Her guides or whatever told her things. And so far, she might have been vague at times, but she'd never been wrong.

I sighed. "Well, Jack and I are headed over to the restaurant again tonight. Maybe we can figure out what Dr. Mickleson was doing there and what, if anything, it has to do with these soul vamps. Other than that, I'm at a loss as to what our next move should be."

"Oh, that's easy," Cordelia said, carefully closing her fan and tucking it away. Her eyes still had that faraway look, and her voice had an odd, hollow sound it sometimes got when she was looped into the other side. It made my skin crawl.

I cleared my throat a little nervously. "It is?"

"Oh, yes." Her words came out sort of scratchy and whispery.

"Okay, then. What do I do?" I asked...whoever Cordelia was channeling.

"Find the key to the key."

***

Find the key to the key? Was Cordelia serious? Talk about clear as mud. My chat with her had been about as useful as wings on a fish. Apart from flying fish, which are freakish.

I shook my head and focused on the task at hand. The last thing we needed was to get caught by the police or Dr. Mickleson, should he happen to stop by. The restaurant door stood just outside the pool of light cast by the nearest streetlight, but anyone walking past could easily see us.

"Would you hurry up?" I hissed.

"Would you like to do it?" Jack snapped without turning his head. He was kneeling in front of the door, tool set in hand, while I held a flashlight. His worn jeans rode low on his hips and his jacket shifted up a little. I tried not to stare at the smooth strip of tanned skin they revealed. I felt guilty for noticing. I felt double guilty for remembering how it felt to caress that tanned skin.

"Not really, no." If the cops wandered by, I'd need all the head start I could get.

"Fine. Then shut up and let me work." He turned his attention back to lock picking, and I turned my attention to giving him the finger behind his back.

"Want to do that to my face?" He snarled. Man, he was testy tonight.

"I'd be happy to. Tell me to shut up again, and it'll be more than my finger you'll be dealing with."

He let out a string of curses in what I could only guess was medieval French as he worked. I wasn't sure if he was cussing out me or the lock. Probably both. Inigo would have had the door open in a matter of seconds. He was a genius with lock picks.

My heart gave a little throb of pain at the thought. Pressing my hand to my breast bone, I willed the ache to subside. I missed Inigo so much, it was less painful to avoid thinking about him. Easier said than done.

"Got it." Jack sounded ridiculously pleased with himself.

"Careful." I nodded toward the small sign in the window that proclaimed the property was guarded by Xeno Security. "Don't want that thing going off."

"I can fix it."

I raised my eyebrows. It wasn't that I doubted him. Okay, I doubted him.

The restaurant door swung open, revealing dark shadows beyond.

"Wait here." Jack stepped through the doorway and disappeared inside while I clicked off the flashlight and kept to the shadows.

I waited for the shriek of an alarm, but nothing happened. Apparently, Jack really could fix it.

Jack reappeared and beckoned me inside. The door swung shut behind us, cutting off some of the light from outside. Inside, it was quiet, still, and a little stuffy, with a strong odor of garlic.

I moved cautiously toward the back of the room where Mickleson had disappeared earlier that day. True, my night vision was superior to that of normal humans, but the last thing I wanted to do was crash into a chair or table. My feet stuck to the floor a little as I walked. Evidently cleanliness was not a top priority. I made a note to never, ever eat at this restaurant.

We passed through the swinging door into the kitchen. Without windows, it was even darker back here. The only lights were from the dim green glow of the exit sign and the tiny emergency light next to it. Below them was a heavy fire door with a steel crash bar. Next to that was a regular door.

I moved closer to the doors, Jack hot on my heels. The second door was a cheap wooden thing with a regular brass-painted doorknob and a seriously complicated looking deadbolt which required a key. Crap.

"Don't worry. I can crack it." Jack said.

"In less than three hours?" I might have been exaggerating slightly.

It was Jack's turn to give me the finger. "Step back."

I moved out of the way, leaning against one of the metal shelving units crammed with an assortment of pots and pans. I expected Jack to pull out the lock picks. Instead, he gave the door one hell of a kick. I heard a loud cracking sound as the door splintered away from the frame, swinging drunkenly on a single hinge.

"Very nice." I gave him a golf clap.

Jack executed a small bow, his full lips quirking into a half smile. "Thank you. Thank you very much."

"That is the worst Elvis impression I've ever heard."

"I'm heartbroken."

"Don't you think someone is going to notice the door's been kicked in?"

Jack shrugged. "By then, we'll have found whatever it is we came to see. Shall we?" He motioned to the open doorway and the stairs descending downward.

"Guardians first." I figured if Jack wanted to play the Guardian card every five minutes, the least he could do was put his ass on the line once in a while. Okay, that wasn't fair. He'd put said ass on the line many times for me and my friends. Still, I had no intention of going down those stairs first.

With another shrug, he slowly descended the stairs. I had a really bad feeling this basement held more than cobwebs and old wine bottles. I took a deep breath and followed him down.

Chapter 19

With the basement door shut behind us, Jack switched on his flashlight. Its harsh white glow revealed a set of rickety wooden steps leading down to a concrete floor. We moved cautiously, the stairs creaking in protest under our combined weight. I probably should cut down on those donuts. Like that was going to happen.

Once we reached the floor, Jack swung his light around, revealing a perfectly ordinary basement. Cobwebs hung from the single bare bulb gracing the ceiling, and a web of cracks and chips from decades of use spread across the floor, marring the concrete. A few cases of various alcoholic beverages were stacked against one wall. In another corner, a dusty sheet covered what appeared to be old dining room chairs and tables. There was nothing here that would have been of interest to a man like Mickleson. He clearly wasn't using the basement.

"Do you feel a draft?" Jack snagged my attention.

I licked my finger and held it up. I'd seen it done in TV shows. Sure enough, I could feel a slight coolness against one side of my finger. Casting my gaze in that direction, I saw nothing but stacks of chairs draped in sheeting. One corner of the grimy cloth stirred slightly.

"There." I pointed toward the corner. "I bet there's something behind those chairs."

Jack kept the flashlight trained on the corner while I moved closer to inspect the stack, one hand on the hilt of my dagger. "I found something."

Sure enough, the chairs had been carefully stacked just far enough away from the wall to allow a person to slip behind them. Smack dab in the middle of the wall was a piece of plywood covering up what appeared to be a fairly large hole. I pulled out my flashlight and played it over the plywood.

"It looks like a hidden exit."

Jack peered around the stacks of chairs. "Or entrance. I'll check it out."

I let him past as he handed me his flashlight. Jack slid the plywood out of the way, revealing the hole. He took back his flashlight and shone it around. "Not much to see. Just another room from the looks of it." He stood up. "Ladies first."

"Chicken." Making a face, I ducked through the opening and into the room beyond.

It wasn't a room, after all. It was a tunnel. Narrow and low with crumbling brick walls and a ceiling of thick crossbeams. The floor was simple packed dirt. The cobwebs were even thicker here. It looked like this section of the Shanghai Tunnels hadn't been used in centuries, but there was no doubt in my mind Mickleson had come this way. Call it a gut instinct.

Jack had to squat in order to maneuver his large frame through the low opening. He nearly whacked his head against one of the crossbeams as he stood up.

"Careful. I don't think they had guys over six feet in mind when they built this place." I doubted they'd had personal space in mind, either. There wasn't enough room for the two of us in the narrow tunnel. Jack was way closer than I'd have liked, his broad shoulders and wide chest crowding me. My breath came a little faster and my heart beat kicked into high gear. Gods dammit, what was wrong with me?

I gave myself a mental shake. This was ridiculous. What Jack and I once had was over. Granted, it had been his choice, not mine, and yeah, I might still find him attractive, but we were partners of a sort. That was it. Coworkers, nothing more. The man I loved was lying in a coma somewhere in Scotland.

And yet something told me things with Jack weren't as settled as I'd like to believe. The thought freaked me out.

"This way." I moved down the tunnel, ignoring Jack and the multitude of problems his presence gave me.

I swiped a cobweb off my cheek, cringing at the clingy stickiness of it. Gross. I hoped any spiders that had once been in that web were long gone. My skin crawled at the thought they might not be. Gods, I hated spiders.

The tunnel ended at another large hole in the wall. This entrance was original, with a carefully crafted archway above and a couple of stone steps that took us down into another basement. This one looked like it had been abandoned for years. The stone floor was coated in a thick layer of dust, and in that dust I saw a trail of footprints leading across the floor and disappearing behind a door at the opposite side of the room.

Mickleson. Had to be.

"Let's see what's behind door number two." I grabbed hold of the cold iron handle and pulled. The heavy wooden door swung open easily. "These hinges have been oiled recently."

Jack nodded. "Mickleson, or somebody, has been coming down here on a regular basis."

The doorway led to another tunnel similar to the first, except there were fewer cobwebs and a little more head room. About ten feet down, we hit an intersection. The tunnel stretched on into darkness, but there was also a branch heading right and another one going left. It was impossible to make out footprints in the hard-packed dirt.

"Crap. Now where?"

Jack shrugged. "No idea. Guess we try them all."

"Left first?"

He nodded his approval. "I'll go right and we'll meet back here."

"Roger that."

I went down the left tunnel, swinging my light back and forth so as not to miss a hidden door or something. There was nothing. The tunnel dead-ended at a cave-in. A huge pile of rubble blocked the path completely. There was no way Mickleson could have gotten through that mess without looking like Charlie Brown's friend, Pigpen. He'd come out of the restaurant a little sweaty but otherwise pristine. He also hadn't been gone long enough to have spent any length of time mucking around. He'd gotten in and gotten out. Hurrying back down the tunnel to the intersection, I waited for Jack. His flashlight came bobbing back toward me a couple minutes later.

"Any luck?"

"There were a couple doors, one of them led into another empty room and the other led to an underground parking garage. Neither door has been opened recently. You?"

"Cave-in. Guess it's straight down the middle."

We continued down the tunnel to another door. Again, it looked ancient, but I could see a few dark spots in the dirt under the hinges.

Jack squatted down and rubbed some of the earth between his fingers. "Oil. This door has been used and recently, too."

"Jackpot."

I twisted the doorknob but it didn't move. Not exactly a surprise. I'd bet anything this was where Mickleson was getting his groove on. "Think you can pick it?"

Jack eyed the lock. "Probably. Here. Hold the flashlight."

I took it from him and stepped back to give Jack room to work. Before I could open my mouth, Jack had rammed his shoulder into the door, which sprang open with a splintering crack. It wasn't nearly as impressive the second time around, but I couldn't help the little thrill I felt at all the macho. Dust sifted down from overhead, sprinkling his head and shoulders as he pushed through the open doorway.

I swung my flashlight beam around, revealing piles of smashed up equipment. It was electronics that looked like it belonged in a hospital or scientific lab. Trays of medical instruments were scattered around, some stamped into the dirt floor. A gurney lay on its side, the thin mattress ripped to shreds. Whatever had been going on, someone was trying to destroy it. Maybe to cover it up. Maybe just because they were mad.

"What the hell?" Jack's voice echoed in the large room.

I grabbed his arm. "Shhh."

His face was a mask of confusion. "What..."

"We're not alone." Pressure gripped the back of my skull: my early warning signal.

From deeper inside the room, two glowing red eyes stared back at us. All three of us stood frozen for a split second. Then the vampire charged.

Chapter 20

At the last possible second, the vampire dodged Jack and hit me full on. I'd like to say I was ready for the bastard, but I'd honestly been expecting him to attack Jack. Or just get the hell out of Dodge. I wasn't as prepared as I should have been. I didn't even have time to pull out a knife. Score one for the vamp.

The force threw me backward, taking me to the floor before I could so much as blink. I landed on my back with a jarring *thud*, the vamp heavy on top of me, as my flashlight skittered away into the blackness. My breath left my lungs in a *whoosh*. I coughed, gasping for air as dark lights danced in front of my eyes. For a moment, eerie red eyes stared into mine. The vampire was under someone else's control. That much was obvious. But there was one other thing: the vampire had a soul.

Before I could do more than register the thought, the vampire started to clamber off me. Apparently he was more interested in escape than ripping my throat out, but I couldn't let him get away. He was our only lead. We needed him in order to find out what Mickleson was up to. So I did the only thing I could think of. I wrapped my legs tight around his waist and held on for dear life.

With a hiss, the vamp back-handed me across the face, smacking my head against the floor. Thank the gods it was dirt, not concrete, or I might have been in serious trouble. I tried to hit him back, but dazed from the blow and lack of oxygen, I only managed to glance a fist off his shoulder. Still, I kept my thighs clamped around him like a vise, using every last ounce of energy I had to hold on.

He cocked his fist to slam my face again, but Jack caught his arm before he connected. There was a sickening crack as Jack twisted the vampire's arm behind his back. Letting out a screech of pain, the vamp threw himself backward so hard, it was either let him go or suffer two broken legs. I let go.

He was off me and headed back through the tunnel before Jack or I could react. I could hear his footsteps fading even as Jack ran after him.

I slowly climbed to my feet, propping myself up against the wall. My fingers scraped against the crumbling bricks, and my nose tickled with the musty, earthy scent. My head swam until I almost upchucked into the corner. The hit had taken a lot more out of me than it should have. I guess, I wasn't entirely back to normal.

Dragging in a deep breath and willing my stomach to behave, I followed the two men through the tunnels. I'd like to say I dashed along behind them in an elegant and sexy manner, like those action heroines in the movies. But it was more like an awkward stagger accompanied by the occasional crash into a wall. I'd be lucky if I made it out without breaking my neck. My night vision was all but useless with my head swimming, so I did the only thing I could think of. I called the Darkness.

From within me, I felt it rise, lifting its head and sniffing the air like a dog. Eagerly, it heaved up and out of that place deep within me. If it had been brighter, I would have been able to see my own vision dimming, tunneling down to a pinprick. As it was, I couldn't see any such thing in the black of the underground, but I knew the minute the Darkness took over. I could suddenly see almost as well as if it were day, except everything was tinged a weird bluish purple.

Even better, my brain stopped spinning and my stomach settled. My equilibrium returned, the power of the Darkness repairing, or at least masking, whatever damage the vamp had done.

I picked up speed, racing around a corner and through a door that was dangling precariously from its hinges. The Darkness giggled, the sound spilling out of my mouth. It was excited by the chase. Frankly, so was I. I could feel the Darkness reaching out to take control, but I held it back with a metaphorical vise grip. I needed it, yes, but I wasn't about to let it take over.

I dashed around another corner, following that grip of pressure on the back of my skull that told me a vampire was near. I could make out Jack a few feet ahead, his body heat shimmering orange and gold against the bluish light of my vision. I could hear his heart pounding and smell the tang of his sweat against the musty earth of the tunnel. The vamp was a little ahead of him. He showed up the same purplish color as the walls of the tunnel. No body heat. Big surprise. He smelled of death and decay and something else, something I couldn't quite put my finger on.

We were almost on him. Just a little farther. I pushed myself, lengthening my stride.

I was within a few feet of Jack when the vamp reached out and yanked something out of the wall. It was hard to tell, but it looked like a branch or stick or something. Jack didn't even pause, just pushed harder, but I hesitated. Under my feet, I felt a rumbling.

"Jack."

It was too late. Next thing I knew, the ceiling caved in.

I ducked instinctively, covering the back of my head and neck as hundreds of pounds of dirt, stones, and gods knew what else crashed to the ground all around me. The tunnel shook with the impact, nearly knocking me off my feet.

When the shaking stopped, the air was so thick with dust, I could hardly breathe. I tucked my face under the collar of my T-shirt, hiding my nose and mouth like a little kid as I coughed up a lungful of dirt. Hopefully the shirt would filter the air enough to keep me from choking to death. I wished I had my sunglasses. The crap in the air was irritating my eyes, but it didn't stop me from realizing I couldn't see the glow from Jack's flashlight anymore, or the orange shimmer of his body heat.

"Jack?" My voice was muffled slightly by my T-shirt. There was no answer. "Jack!" A little louder this time.

Still nothing. Not even my Darkness-enhanced hearing helped. I searched the area visually, willing the Darkness to pick up Jack's heat signature. No such luck. Not so much as a faint glow penetrated the thick blackness of the tunnel.

"Dammit, Jack, answer me."

He didn't. Shit. He must have been far enough ahead of me to get caught in the cave-in. The pile of rubble was so enormous, it would take days for me to dig through it. I had no idea how deep in he was or even in which direction. If I dug in the wrong place...

Panic threatened to overwhelm me, but I told myself not to be a ninny. Jack had a habit of dying and coming back to life, thanks to his connection to me and the Atlantis amulet.

The amulet.

I pulled it out from under my shirt. For once, I was glad I'd listened to Jack and started wearing it. Maybe it would help me find him under the mess. It was a long shot, but I had to try.

I cradled the Heart of Atlantis in my palm. The smooth metal was warm from my skin, the center stone dark and lifeless. I could just make out the faint etchings of Atlantean hieroglyphs circling the edge of the disc. Focusing on the stone, I brought Jack's image to the forefront of my mind's eye. I had no idea if it would work, but I followed my instincts.

I'm not sure what I expected, but nothing happened. At least not at first. Then the stone began to glow, bathing the tunnel in soft blue light. Holy crap. It only did that when Sidhe magic was near.

"Morgana?" I whispered. Any help she gave would have strings attached, but I'd do it for Jack. For anyone I loved, really, but Jack had sacrificed himself for me more than once; I owed him.

Unfortunately, there was no answer. Instead the stone dimmed.

"Dammit." I focused again and once more the stone began to glow. "Okay, now what?" As if it would answer me.

I moved closer to the pile of rubble, and the glow intensified. Now we were getting somewhere. Shifting to the right, I noticed the light from the stone dimmed. To the left, it got brighter. That had to be where Jack was. Apparently the amulet wanted me to play a game of Hide the Thimble, only Jack was the thimble and the brighter the light, the closer I was.

Tucking the Heart back in my shirt, I decided I'd worry about the how of it later. I reached out and grabbed the nearest chunk of rock. Even with my extra-human strength and an assist from the Darkness, heaving the rock off the rubble pile took some doing. A few more rocks and my back was aching, the muscles in my arms trembling, and sweat had soaked through my clothes.

The Darkness couldn't hide my headache any longer, either. My head throbbed with pain until I felt sick and dizzy.

I sank down to the tunnel floor. This was going to take forever. Maybe channeling one of my other powers would help. I shook my head at my own foolishness. Fire would eat up the oxygen and that was about it. It was less than useless. Ditto with Air. I so did not need a whirlwind kicking up a bunch of dust.

And then I nearly smacked myself upside the head. I was an idiot. What had Tommy been working on with me for an entire week? And the reason my amulet had been glowing like there were Sidhe lurking in the corners? Thanks to Morgana dragging me to the other world, I had a brand new shiny superpower: Earth.

I had no idea how to use my power exactly. I doubted causing an earthquake or growing weeds was going to be helpful, but there had to be something I could do.

I reached out and laid my palm against the pile of dirt and stone. Closing my eyes, I focused on that place inside me where my powers lurked. Waiting. Waiting.

Underneath the dainty ribbons of Air and Fire, and the undulating bands of Darkness, I found that shimmering green ribbon. I beckoned to it, asking it to come out and play. It rose in loops and waves, unfurling like a cat from a long nap. Or maybe like a sentient vine.

Unlike the Air and Fire, which always seemed to shoot out of me like laser beams, the Earth slowly unfurled, rising through me like mist. It seeped through my pores, covering my skin in a layer of sparkly green visible only to me and anyone else with magic in their veins.

I showed the Earth power an image of Jack trapped under the debris. Then I showed it an image of Jack being freed from the debris. I felt kind of dumb, but it was the best I had.

I dug my fingers into the pile of rubble and willed something to happen. At first, nothing did. Then the dirt under my fingers began to sift away like the parting of the Red Sea. Stone, dirt, and wood peeled back until they finally revealed what I was looking for.

Jack lay curled in a fetal position, covered from head to toe in dirt and something else. From the copper tang in the air, I knew it was blood.

I crawled into the gap next to Jack and laid my fingers against his throat to check for a pulse. Not that a pulse or lack thereof meant much where Jack was concerned. As I touched his bare skin, green light shot from my hand into him, bathing him in the same green sparkles that covered my body. I had no idea what they were doing, but it felt right.

So, I sat there and waited.

***

"What happened?"

A pair of eyes the color of a tropical ocean stared at me from a dirty face. Relief overwhelmed me. Tears pricked the corners of my eyes, and I felt the sudden urge to hug Jack tight and plant a huge kiss on those dirty lips. Instead, I backed off slightly, rubbing my suddenly damp palms on my jeans.

"Vamp set off some kind of booby trap. Buried you under half the ceiling." I backed out of the narrow gap in the rubble before standing and offering him my hand. Ignoring me, he staggered to his feet. Arrogant bastard. "Good thing you're immortal or you'd be a pancake right about now."

He snorted. "The vamp?"

"Got away."

"You didn't go after him?"

His accusatory tone made me want to punch him in the face. Or somewhere more delicate. "Excuse me, but I was busy saving your sorry ass. Besides, he cut me off pretty effectively." I waved at the enormous pile of crap blocking the tunnel.

"There are a lot of ways out of the tunnels."

"Right. And with no idea where he ended up, not to mention being entirely unfamiliar with the tunnels, all of those exits would be damn useless. Don't be an asshat, Jack."

"Sorry."

He didn't sound particularly sorry. He sounded like he wanted to argue some more, but I ignored him. I wasn't worried about the vampire getting away. I could always hunt him down later. It was what I did. I changed the subject. "I think we should go back and check out that room. The one with all the medical stuff. There might be something there, something that whoever smashed the place up missed."

"You mean that the vamp smashed up," Jack said.

His correction made me grind my teeth in irritation. "We don't know that," I said, heading back down the tunnel. "Maybe he did, or maybe it was Mickleson, earlier." Though I doubted that. There hadn't been enough time for Mickleson to smash all that stuff. My bet was he'd come here to warn someone. "Or maybe it was somebody else."

The room was exactly as we'd left it: dark and littered with junk. Tables were overturned, a chair lay on its side in the corner, and there were several computers that looked like they'd been on the wrong end of a sledgehammer. I've felt like taking a hammer to my computer on more than one occasion, but I doubted these were smashed because somebody got pissed off at Microsoft.

I found my flashlight in the corner still intact. With a sigh of relief I switched it on and began exploring the remains of the makeshift lab.

Something crunched under my boot. Squatting to check it out, I held up a bit of glass to my flashlight. "Hard to tell, but it looks like test tubes. Maybe microscope slides or petri dishes."

"Yeah. This definitely looks like something off CSI." Jack held up the remains of a badly dented centrifuge.

I stood and scanned the room with my flashlight. "What the hell were they doing down here? Were they studying something? Creating something?"

"Not to mention, who are 'they?'"

Something in the corner caught my eye. I strode over and picked up a fragment of paper that had been ground almost completely into the dirt floor. Turning it over in my hands, I smiled.

"I think I might have the answer to that."

"What do you mean?"

Holding the paper up, I shined the light behind it, illuminating what was left of the watermark. "Look at that symbol there."

Jack frowned. "Yeah. It's a watermark. So?"

"It's not just any watermark. That's the family crest of Alister Jones."

Chapter 21

"Vampires have souls now, thanks to Alister? You've got to be kidding me." I noticed Kabita didn't say "my father" as she paced the confines of her office. Angry energy rolled off her in waves, and I winced as my powers reacted to it. They liked anger. It made them stronger.

I sighed as I sank into the buttery-soft visitor's chair, ignoring the pull inside me. "I wish I was."

"And what? He's kidnapping old people and turning them into vamps?"

"Jack and I don't think so. As far as we can tell, he's transferring the souls of the dying elderly into the bodies of existing vampires." At least that's what we'd put together based on what Tommy had told me of the technology, and our own observations. It really was the only thing that made sense. Even turning vampire wouldn't make an elderly person young again.

Kabita sat on the edge of her desk, jiggling one black jean-clad leg. Her cinnamon skin looked a little paler than usual. "That's sick. Why on earth would they do that?"

"We know a vampire can't be made without losing its soul, and it seems a soul can't be captured until the moment it leaves the body. Our best guess is that capturing dying souls and inserting them into existing vamps is the only way to imbue a vampire with a soul." It sounded totally insane even to me.

Kabita started pacing again, her black biker boots thumping slightly on the thick beige carpet.

She'd been on a demon hunt and hadn't bothered to change. "And again I ask, why?"

"We assume to make the vampires easier to control. Beyond that? No idea." I shook my head. "We're working on it."

"Fantastic," Kabita snarled. She glared at the wastebasket next to her desk like she wanted to do it bodily harm. She didn't. She had far more restraint than I did. Points to Kabita. "What else can go wrong?"

Besides me dreaming of the Fairy Queen torturing Jade, Inigo being in a weird dragon coma, Brent Darroch escaping from an inescapable prison, and Cordelia giving me cryptic messages from beyond? "Uh, have I mentioned someone has a hit out on me?"

Kabita smacked her forehead. "For goddess's sake, Morgan." Her tone had a very "why me" quality to it. Couldn't say I blamed her.

"Sorry. Just thought I could figure it out on my own. No sense worrying anybody else." I'd yet to make any headway in that department; I'd been a little busy with other things.

She kicked out her desk chair and threw herself into it, which was about as close to a temper tantrum as Kabita ever came. "You seriously couldn't have mentioned this earlier? Like, oh, say, before you got nearly ripped to shreds by some vampire chick who fancied herself a bounty hunter?"

I opened my mouth, but I didn't have time to get anything out before Kabita barreled on. "Why is it that you insist on going off half-cocked, marching into danger with your eyes closed?"

"Hey, that's not true." Well, not entirely. I had been going off the rails a little lately. But I was working on it. Honest.

Kabita just glared at me. Then her dark eyes widened. "Oh, goddess, it's Alister, isn't it?"

"Uh, what is?" Color me clueless.

"The hit. Alister ordered the hit on you." She said it with such conviction, she almost had me believing.

"It's possible," I admitted. "But we really don't know. Inigo..." My heart gave a painful lurch at the thought of him. I cleared my throat. "Inigo couldn't trace the IP and none of the vamps I've had the pleasure of dusting have bothered to share any insight with me. So, we don't really know anything for sure. Could be him. Could be somebody else. I've pissed off a few people over the years." Understatement of the century.

"Bullshit. It's Alister. Has to be."

Things were serious if Kabita was cussing. I had a bad feeling she was right. There were a handful of people who would be happy to see me dead. Alister Jones was top of the list.

Kabita's phone jangled. She pulled it out of her pocket and frowned at the caller ID before answering. "Yeah? Uh huh? Where? Sure. Yeah, I can do that."

I raised my eyebrows as she hung up. "That was all kinds of mysterious."

"It was Jack. He wants me to talk to the SRA."

"What does Jack want with the SRA?" Jack preferred staying far under their radar for obvious reasons. The SRA did not have a good track record where Atlantean descendants were concerned, and Jack was more than your average Atlantean. Why hadn't he mentioned anything to me before? Like maybe while we were wandering around a bunch of underground tunnels?

"Apparently," Kabita said, sinking into her chair, "he has the sudden urge to travel."

I blinked. "What?"

"He asked me to secure him a private jet."

***

"Jack, you got some 'splaining to do." I might have channeled a tiny bit of Desi Arnaz. Might as well keep a bit of humor about the situation. I could do full-on confrontation if I had to, but more flies with honey, and all that.

"What are you talking about?" Jack's voice on the other end of the line had all the overtones of innocence, but underneath was something else. He had definitely been hiding something from me.

I headed down the front stairs of our office building and across the parking lot to my car. "A private plane? Really? What on earth do you need a private plane for?" I asked as I slid into my Mustang.

"Do you not understand the meaning of the word 'private'?"

I ignored his royal snippiness. "Does this have anything to do with what we found in the tunnels? With Alister?"

"No."

I didn't say anything. I snapped my seatbelt, turned on the ignition, and waited.

"Okay, fine. Maybe," he sighed. I could visualize him running his hands through his hair in frustration. He did that around me a lot. Couldn't imagine why.

"And you planned to tell me when?" I asked.

"This side of never," he mumbled.

"Excuse me?"

"When I knew for sure." Back to innocence.

"Yeah, okay. Whatever. Do I need a passport?" I was pissed as hell at him for leaving me out of the loop after dragging me into this mess in the first place, but damned if I was going to let him know it.

A pause. "What?"

"I'm going with you." If he thought I was staying behind while he jaunted off to solve the mystery of the soul vampires, he had another think coming.

Another pause. "Morgan."

"You know I'm not taking no for an answer, Jack, and if you refuse to tell me, I'll just figure it out and follow you."

"Fine." He let out another exasperated sigh. "Yes. You'll need a passport."

"Cool. Where are we going?"

"France."

***

"So," I said, settling back against the plush leather seats of the private plane Kabita had arranged. When she and I traveled, we usually went first class, but this was so far beyond that, it was ridiculous. "Why France?"

Jack took a sip of his whiskey on the rocks and stared out the little oval window as if the tarmac were the most interesting thing in the universe. "It's where I'm from."

I rolled my eyes and opened my mouth to retort, but I was interrupted by the flight attendant. She handed me an icy glass of fizzy golden liquid from her silver tray before disappearing through a wood-paneled door at the back of the plane. I took a cautious sip. Pear cider. The good stuff. Delicious. How on earth had she known it was my favorite? I took a few more sips before returning to the conversation.

"Yes, I know that's where you're from," I said, setting my glass cautiously on a little side table. "Most Templar Knights were from France. I get that." I knew Jack had been another person, had another life, but that was nine-hundred-years ago, give or take a few decades. He'd spent the last several centuries as an American, and the centuries before that in Scotland. "But what's so important you need to take off right this minute for France?"

He took another sip of whiskey. He still hadn't looked at me. Not since I'd embarked on the plane with an overnight duffel and my turquoise rolly bag stuffed with weaponry.

"You know about the night the Templars were destroyed?" he said finally.

"Friday the Thirteenth, 1307." Some said that was when the whole bad luck superstition thing came from. "The King of France slaughtered nearly all the Templars. The rest, he arrested and publicly executed after forcing them to confess to everything from hanky panky with each other to consorting with the devil." King Phillip had been a power hungry rat bastard. He'd couched the slaughter in religious terms, of course, but it had really been all about two things: money and power. The Templars had both, and the king wanted them.

"More or less." Jack nodded. "There were some who got away."

"Including you."

He shrugged. "Actually, I left several months before that. I guess the leaders of the order could sense change in the wind."

"Right. You hid out near the coast, and then went to Scotland. You told me all this before."

"Before that, though, I stopped in a tiny French village where people were sympathetic to our cause. I hid something there. Something I'd been entrusted with." He took another sip of whiskey.

I frowned. I'd known about the amulet. Hell, I was wearing it around my neck. I fingered its chain. "There's more than this?"

"Oh, yes," he said, his eyes darkening to the stormy blue gray of the Pacific Ocean in winter. "Much more."

"And we're going to France to get it?"

His expression was grim. "No. We're going to France because someone stole it. We're going to find out who took it and get it back."

Chapter 22

Soft lips pressed against my throat, skimming gently up to the sensitive spot behind my ear. Heat unfurled as a palm cupped my breast, kneading gently. Aroused, I pressed up against the solid body of the man holding me in his arms.

"Ah, love, I've missed you." His voice was hoarse, as if he hadn't used it in awhile.

"Inigo?" The joy that flooded me was beyond describing. Tears welled in my eyes, swelling my throat tight as I cupped his cheeks in my hands, holding his head away so I could drink in every curve and plane of his beautiful face.

Sapphire-blue eyes stared back at me, heavy with desire. Lush lips curved in a smile. "Who else." His low, sexy chuckle sent my hormones and my heart zinging happily. Who else indeed?

With excruciating slowness, he undid my shirt, one button at a time. He pressed a kiss to each inch of skin he revealed, as though he were savoring the taste of me. I tangled my hands in his hair, letting the silky strands slide through my fingers as I guided him down, down...

He stopped at my waistband, and I let out a sound of frustration.

He chuckled again. "Patience, love."

"Not my strong suit."

His grin was infectious. "Don't I know it." *Slowly, he kissed his way back up to my collarbone, sliding my shirt off my shoulders to toss it on the floor. He kissed my throat, my jawline, before settling his mouth over mine in one of those slow, hot kisses that left me feeling drugged.*

His tongue slid and danced over mine. I lost myself in the wet heat of his mouth, and the scent of campfires and s'mores that was uniquely Inigo. I slid my hands over his hot skin, memorizing every inch.

"You were gone. You left me." I couldn't help it. All the pain and sorrow suddenly came welling out. Wounds ripped open by passion.

"Never," he whispered against my lips. "Never. I'm always with you Morgan. Every minute of every day. I promise you that."

"You make it sound like you're dead," I choked out, a salty tear threatening to spill over and slide down my cheek.

"Do I feel dead to you?" He pressed himself into me until I could feel the hard length of his arousal.

"Hells, no." My voice was a little strangled.

"Good." His expression turned serious again, focused on the task at hand.

With one hand, he flicked open my purple bra before pushing me down on the bed. The lacy confection joined my shirt on the floor.

"Perfect," he whispered as he cupped my heavy breasts in his palms.

Every woman should have a man who believes with every fiber of his being that she is beautiful. I slid my hands to the hem of his T-shirt, wanting to feel his bare skin against mine. To see his own perfection.

"Not yet."

He pulled my hands away, and then lowered his mouth to my left breast. Drawing my nipple into his mouth, he flicked it with his tongue. Heat shot straight to my core. I arched my back, wanting more.

He obliged, drawing my nipple into the hot wetness of his mouth.

He moved to my other breast, repeating the process. He sucked and licked until I was so wet and wanting, I thought I'd come from that alone.

He slid a hand to my waist, popping the button on my jeans and lowering the zipper tab. I wriggled a little, helping him as he pulled my jeans and panties slowly down my thighs and off, tossing them off the bed.

Wanting him naked, I grabbed the soft hem of his shirt again, pulling it up and over. It joined my clothes in a tangled pool on the floor, but he wouldn't let me touch his jeans. "Not yet."

I groaned in frustration. "Jerk." I said it with more affection than malice. His laugh rumbled against my sensitized skin.

He caressed my stomach and lower, stroking, parting me. He slid his fingers through my wetness. "Oh, gods, Morgan."

His fingers swirled around my bud. I whimpered at his touch as little tremors shot through me.

Our kiss was so hot, I thought we'd both go up in flames. This time he let me take off his jeans and black boxer briefs. Finally.

He took me in one long, slow slide. Stretching, filling. Little mini orgasms shot through me. I dug my fingers into the thick muscles of his shoulders, a whimper building in the back of my throat.

He pulled out, almost to the tip, before thrusting back in. Hard. I arched to take him as deep as I could, letting out something between a scream and a groan at the sheer pleasure. I'd never been a quiet lover.

We fell into a rhythm, each thrust sending us closer and closer to the edge. One more, and we toppled over. Our cries of ecstasy were music to my ears.

As the afterglow faded, I held him tight in my arms, afraid to let him go lest I wake up and realize it was all a dream. "Gods I've missed this."

"Me, too." His voice was muffled. One hand was clenched in my hair and the other wrapped around me, holding me close.

I stroked his hair and down his neck to the smooth skin of his back. "I've missed you."

"Why? I've been right here." He raised his head, and the face staring back at me wasn't Inigo's. It was Jack.

***

I came awake with a gasp, kicking and thrashing at the thin blanket which had managed to somehow wrap around my legs. I flailed, half out of it, until I realized I'd been dreaming after all. I hadn't just made love. I was on a plane. Headed to France. With Jack.

Jack.

Oh, gods.

I buried my face in my hands, feeling a little ill. How could I dream of two men like this? I must have something wrong with my head.

"You okay?" Jack glanced over from his seat on the other side of the plane. He was holding a book, one of those Dan Brown type thrillers, and looked only vaguely interested in my condition.

"Huh?"

"Looks like you had a bad dream."

I swallowed, heat rising in my cheeks as I shoved hair out of my face. "Something like that. Where are we?"

"We'll be landing in about thirty minutes."

I nodded. "Guess I've got time to powder my nose."

I jumped up and rushed to the bathroom. Jack shot me a baffled look as I slammed the door behind me. I braced myself over the sink, half afraid I might be ill.

I felt guilty. Like I'd actually just cheated on Inigo, even though it had only been a stupid, ridiculous dream. And we can't control our dreams, right? I would never do that in real life. Besides, Cordelia had told me not to put too much stock in these dreams of Jack and Inigo. But what was I to think when I kept dreaming of them both?

I knew it was ridiculous to get so worked up over a dream, but I couldn't help it. It had all been so *real*. I was still half aroused and completely wracked with guilt and confusion.

"Get a grip," I snarled at my reflection before splashing my face with cold water. I ran wet fingers through my hair, trying to wrestle it back into some semblance of respectability.

It was just a dream, probably brought on by the fact that it had been several months since I'd had sex. Not to mention my boyfriend was in a coma, or whatever you want to call that weird egg thing, and my life was a total disaster at the moment. The dream didn't mean anything. Except that maybe I needed to get my head examined.

Chapter 23

The French countryside stretched out on either side of the car, wild with daffodils and the pink and white fuzz of tree blossoms. Here and there, stone farmhouses dotted the landscape, colorful wooden shutters open to the morning sun. Despite the cool temperature, I had the window cracked so I could catch the fresh air. The wind teased at my hair and chilled my skin, leaving me grateful I'd thought to wear my leather jacket. For a moment, I could almost pretend this was just a vacation and it was Inigo driving the car, not Jack.

I cast a sideways glance at Jack. As if I didn't have every plane of his face lodged in my mind for eternity. If I were honest with myself, in a way I was glad it was him I was with. I had been so angry with him, and yet I had missed him, too. It felt good to be back on the hunt together, and that gave me yet another thing to feel guilty about. How could I enjoy myself and enjoy time spent with another man when Inigo was...

I forced my thoughts away from their maudlin path and cast my gaze back to the scenery. Willing myself to relax, I tried to recapture my daydreams of holidays and Inigo.

"We're here." Jack's voice interrupted my fantasies. Dammit.

He'd pulled off to the side of the road in front of the world's smallest village. Most of the buildings shared common walls. Only the varying pastel colors on the shutters gave away the fact that they were, indeed, separate dwellings.

I expected villagers to pop their heads out of the open windows to inspect us. Classic behavior in small towns everywhere. But they didn't. If there was anyone home, they were inside, firmly minding their own business.

In the dead center of the village was a small circle of grass with an old pump well in the middle. Once upon a time, it would have been the only source of water for the village. Now it was a curiosity. Charming, but useless. Like that clump of parsley they dump on top of your cheeseburger at restaurants.

On the other side of the town "square" was a small stone church that looked like it had been there for centuries, possibly even longer than the houses. More buildings of indeterminate use lined the village next to the church, their empty windows staring blankly on the world. The village was cute, I'll admit, but there wasn't even a bakery. How did one get fresh croissants in the morning?

Jack hopped out of the Land Rover, slamming the door behind him and startling me out of yet another reverie. What was wrong with me lately?

I hurried to catch up as he strode along the road and across the square toward the church. Okay, that made sense. It had been a priest who had called him, after all, and Jack had been a Templar. Templars and churches sort of went hand in hand.

The inside of the church was dim and silent. The plain, simple plaster walls and high arched ceiling spoke of antiquity. Norman, maybe. I held back a sneeze as the thick, musty air tickled my throat. Between the heavy dampness, unpleasant odor, and the rock-hard benches, I wondered that anyone bothered to come to church.

"Now what?" I stepped up next to Jack, waiting for...well, I had no idea what we were waiting for. There was nothing other than the unlocked front door to indicate anyone had been inside the church in ages.

Jack didn't answer. He just stood there, arms crossed, an aloof expression on his face. I wondered what sort of memories this place held for him. He'd been his usual uncommunicative self the entire ride over from the airport. It was getting on my nerves. Nothing new there.

A stirring toward the front of the church alerted me we weren't alone. I tensed my fingers, reaching for a hidden blade, but Jack seemed unconcerned, so I relaxed. Not entirely, of course. I'm not that dumb. I kept my hand close enough to the knife that I could grab it in an instant.

The man who stepped from the shadows didn't look much like a priest. For one thing, he was dressed in the simple brown robes of a monk instead of the more priestly vestments. For another, he was barefoot, and his long reddish-brown hair was in a queue down his back. His craggy features lightened the minute he saw Jack.

"What kind of a priest is he?" I kept my voice barely above a whisper, knowing Jack could hear me.

"The good kind."

The two men embraced like long-lost brothers, tears in their eyes. There was a lot of back thumping in that way guys do when they're hugging but still want to look macho. I don't think I'd ever seen so much emotion from Jack for another person. Not even me, back when we'd been together, for all he'd accused me of making him weak and distracted.

They spoke in French, or something like it, for a moment, and then Jack turned back to me. "Morgan, I'd like to introduce you to one of my oldest and dearest friends, Father Jean-Pierre. JP, this is Morgan Bailey."

John Peter. Two of the most famous apostles. "The Rock" and "the Beloved." Interesting. Or not. Who knew with priests?

I stepped forward and shook the father's hand. His handshake was warm, firm, and a tingle of power radiated from him. Double interesting. I was pretty sure he was human, but he was tapped into something big, and it wasn't the Church.

"Nice to meet you, Father."

"And you, Ms. Bailey. Jack has told me so much about you," Father Jean-Pierre said.

Wonderful. I can imagine the horror stories Jack told him, but the priest's voice, lightly accented, was sincere and without judgment.

"Please," I said, "call me Morgan."

The priest's smile lit up his face and made him almost handsome. "And you please call me JP. It's what Jack insists on calling me, and I've grown rather fond of it." He laughed, and I couldn't help but join in. I felt myself being sucked under his spell. The priest had a startling way of drawing you into his little cocoon of warmth and friendship. Was it a natural priest thing, or something more?

"Okay, then, JP. Lead on."

He lifted a rusty eyebrow. "Lead on?"

Jack sighed. "I think what Morgan is saying, in her usual abrupt manner, is that she'd like to see the evidence from the break in." He made it sound as if I'd done something rude and embarrassing.

I glared at Jack. Why did he always insist on throwing me under the bus? And just when I was starting to like him again. "I don't see the point in beating around the bush. JP called us for help and we're here. Let's do what we came to do."

"Quite right," JP said with a nod. "If you're going to find who took the book and get it back, we need to move quickly."

"Book?" I hadn't heard anything about a book. Jack had just mentioned something had been stolen. He hadn't been specific, and he had refused to go into detail no matter how much I threatened.

JP glanced at Jack, then back to me. His hazel eyes caught mine and held, as if willing me to understand. "Yes. I will explain everything to you, but first I'd like you to see it with unprejudiced eyes. Please, follow me."

When I nodded, he turned and hurried back up the aisle of the church and across the front area to the right. I admit, I tended to keep out of churches as much as possible so my knowledge of technical terms was pretty limited, apart from apse jokes.

We ducked through a doorway at the side of the church's main room into a tiny chamber that looked like it might be used either as storage or a mud room. On the other side of the chamber was another wooden door, which JP pushed open. It led into a small courtyard surrounded by flower beds, and behind them, a wall of low shrubs. Someone, probably JP, had filled the beds with herbs instead of the usual roses and pansies. Their rich green tang was a welcome relief from the musty interior of the church.

We followed JP across the courtyard to a narrow gap in the shrubbery, where he swung open a wrought iron gate. On the other side of the shrubs lay a wide field with a narrow, muddy footpath winding its way lazily through the rich green grass. The daffodils were so thick, they perfumed the air with their scent. Bees buzzed as they hopped from flower to flower, and birds chirped in the trees a few hundred yards away, down along the river.

Once again, I found myself lost in fantasy, forgetting for a moment we were here on serious business. I could have stayed in that meadow for hours enjoying the scents and sounds of spring, the warm sun on my face, and the faint breeze tugging at my hair. Instead, I hustled along in JP's wake, Jack stomping along behind me.

***

The path meandered along, dipping down by the creek before heading back up the slight hill toward a grove of evergreen trees. I eyeballed the thicket with suspicion. The last time I'd been lured to such a place, it had been to face down the Fairy Queen's psycho brother, Alberich. It hadn't been a particularly fun experience, and not one I wished to repeat. My hand drifted close to my knife again.

What waited for us on the other side of the trees was not a lunatic Sidhe, fortunately. Instead, we found a charming little chapel that looked older than the church. Its stone walls were dark and cracked with age, softened here and there with bits of moss and lichen. The roof was low, many of the slates having been replaced in recent years with brighter red ones that set a jarring note against the dull gray of the older slates. The windows were hardly more than slits high up on the walls, built during a time when glass was almost unheard of.

The narrow path led straight to the chapel door. After fumbling with the ancient lock, JP ushered us inside.

I waited for my eyes to adjust to the darkness. Only tiny trickles of light dared intrude on the sacred space. Dust motes danced in the narrow rays of sunshine. I could feel the zing of energy dancing along my skin. It had nothing to do with religion and everything to do with spirit. And I'm not talking ghosts.

The only piece of furniture in the place was a simple altar at the front of the room. No benches, offering boxes, or fountains here. Not even a cross, which I found unusual.

"Someone broke in?" I asked. "How can you tell?"

JP beckoned us to follow him. "This way."

He strode to the altar with Jack and me hot on his heels. The altar had been carved from a single piece of granite. The only adornment on the otherwise smooth stone was a carving in the front of a double cross: the Cross of Lorraine. It was the symbol of the Knights Templar.

I started to ask about it, but before I could get anything out, JP pressed his fingers along one side of the carving. With a scraping sound that grated against my eardrums, the altar slowly swung to one side, revealing a staircase that descended into the depths of the earth. I stood there with my mouth hanging open as JP and Jack started down the stairs.

Jack turned around and gave me a look of impatience. "Well. Are you coming?"

"I am spending way too much time underground these days," I grumbled as I followed them down into the darkness.

Chapter 24

The stone steps were ancient, worn smooth by thousands of feet over hundreds of years so they dipped awkwardly in the center. I ran my hand along the masonry wall as we descended deeper and deeper. Each stone was perfectly cut and carefully nestled into place without the use of mortar. The work of expert stonemasons. It made sense; Templars were the precursors to the Masons, or so it was said.

And that made me wonder: how many modern day Masons knew the truth? About the world, the supernatural, and the secrets Jack had kept for nearly a millennium. Did they know about Atlantis, for instance? Or the SRA? More to the point, did they know about me?

I shook my head. That was a question for another time. If the modern Masons did know anything, they played it very close to the vest. Couldn't say I blamed them. Could you imagine George Washington running around dusting vampires?

Actually, come to think of it...

My feet finally touched the bottom. In front of me was an intricately carved stone archway, rich with symbols I recognized from documentaries I'd seen on the History Channel. Templar Knights had always been something of an obsession of mine. Too bad Jack had refused to share much of his past. I paused to trace my fingers over roses, double crosses, and more arcane carvings. A few of them looked like they might be Atlantean, or at least Atlantean inspired. Another connection to my ancestry.

Through the archway was a large room. It was a replica of the one above, except instead of the plainness of the upper room, the walls and arches were richly carved in symbols. A secret Templar chapel underneath the public one.

"What is this place?" I asked as JP came to a stop in the center of the room. "I mean, I know it's a Templar chapel, but why all the secrecy? Templars were incredibly powerful and had chapels everywhere. They didn't need to hide underground." Not until that fateful day, Friday the Thirteenth.

"Ah, but the leaders always knew there might come a day when their influence would wane." The priest's expression turned grim. "And there's nothing more endangered than a power whose time is up."

Jack had been unusually quiet during our trip. Not that he was ever very chatty. I wondered how this blast from the past was making him feel. I couldn't even imagine how bizarre it must be.

"Blood on the water," he mumbled under his breath.

No kidding. The entire time the Templars had been in power, the French kings and even the Church had been jealous. The minute the Templars' influence began to fade, King Phillip was all over them like white on rice. And while the Church may not have been quite the culprit some stories had painted it, the pope still hadn't stood in the way of the king's atrocities.

"Okay," I said, turning slowly to take in the room, "I get why this place was important then. But why now?"

"Because it is well hidden," JP explained.

"This book you mentioned. It was here?" I asked.

"Yes. It was the safest place. Or so we thought."

I nodded. It made sense. The chapel was so out-of-the-way it would be nearly impossible to find. But someone had found it anyway.

Jack watched me, his demeanor silent and brooding. He was being singularly unhelpful. Either this was a test, or he was being a jackass. As his former lover, I'd have liked to go with jackass. As the Key of Atlantis, I had a feeling it was a test both of my deductive skills and of whatever supernatural powers had currently taken up residence in my body.

"Where exactly was the book kept?" I asked, glancing around the room. My guess was the altar, since there didn't seem to be any place else to store a book. It just seemed a little dumb to leave it lying about in plain sight.

Father Jean-Pierre stepped behind the altar. He pressed a series of symbols on the wall, and then stepped back as one of the stones popped out. "Here," he said, pulling the stone from the wall and placing it on the altar. "It was kept in this space."

I stepped closer and studied the hidden chamber. It was small. About six or seven inches across, maybe five deep, and with the height of a mail box slot. It would have held something about the size of a pocketbook paperback. Now it was completely empty. Not even a cobweb.

"When did the book go missing?"

"I'm not sure," JP admitted. "The book is old and somewhat fragile. It's best to leave it alone, sealed within the wall. I check on this chapel about once a month to insure things are in order, but I only inspect the book perhaps once in six months to avoid exposing it to the elements." He hesitated. There was something he wasn't saying.

"But this time?"

"I checked early. I got a feeling something was...off. When I looked, I discovered the book was gone." He shrugged. Clearly he was uncomfortable with nebulous feelings, unlike me. I pretty much lived off gut feeling.

"And the last time you did an inspection?"

"Two months ago."

Better than six months, but not by much. The book could be anywhere by now. I figured JP was smart enough to figure that out for himself, so I concentrated on what we did know.

"This had to be an inside job." I kept my voice as matter-of-fact and nonaccusatory as possible. JP looked suitably horrified. Jack leaned against the wall and crossed his arms over his chest, glancing from JP to me and back again.

"Why do you say that?" A muscle worked in the good Father's jaw.

I manage to refrain from rolling my eyes. Was he stupid, or just naive? "Well, let me count the ways. First," I ticked off a finger, "a thief would have to find the chapel above. It's not exactly on the map."

"Tourists do stumble upon it from time to time," JP said.

"True. But," I held up a second finger, "you have to know to mess around with the altar in order to get down here. In fact, you have to know there even is a 'down here' to get to, so either you know where to push or you get really lucky." A third finger. "Once you descend into the belly of the beast, you have to find the right spot on the wall and push the right stones in the right order to reveal the book's hiding place. Finally," I held up a fourth finger, "you have to know there's something here worth taking. This is not something a person stumbles on randomly."

JP's expression didn't change. Jack, however, was watching me like a hawk.

"Who else knows of this chapel?" I asked. "Other than Jack, obviously."

JP nodded. "There is only one other. My predecessor. He is retired now and living in seclusion in Paris. There is no way he would reveal the book's existence, never mind its location."

"But the book has been here a long time."

The two men exchanged looks. Jack finally spoke up. "Since 1307."

The year King Phillip and his minions massacred most of the Templars in France. "And over the years, there have been other caretakers?"

Another glance. Another nod.

"Then someone during the last seven-hundred-plus years could have said something to the wrong person."

"It's possible," JP admitted. His tone told me he thought it unlikely, but I wasn't buying it. People talked, even closemouthed Templars and holy priests. The best kept secrets had a way of finding themselves whispered into the wrong ears.

"Someone other than the three of you could have known what was here and either had the exact set of directions, which is possible though unlikely, or got the information out of one of you three."

"No way." Jack shook his head. "None of us would betray the cause like that."

Not on purpose. I didn't say it aloud, but I'm pretty sure Jack read it on my face. Still, I left it alone for the moment. "The cause? What exactly is this book? Why is it so important?"

Jack and JP shifted uncomfortably. Neither said anything.

"Spill," I ordered. I was getting tired of the game.

"We don't know," Jack finally admitted.

"What do you mean?" How did they not know? They'd been protecting this thing longer than most countries had been in existence.

Jack sighed, running his hands through his shaggy, sun-streaked hair. "We found it in the same cave where we found your amulet."

I blinked. This was the first I'd heard of it. "Wait a minute. That would make the book thousands of years old. Wouldn't it have crumbled to dust by now?"

"It would have," JP spoke up, "if it were made of leather and vellum or cardboard and paper, like most books."

"What on earth is it made of?"

Jack shook his head. "We don't know. Back then we'd never seen anything like it. We still haven't. It's not any material that this world has produced, as near as I can tell."

My eyes widened. "It's from Atlantis."

Jack nodded. "I don't dare have it tested."

That I understood. For one thing, it would mean damaging the book. For another, it would result in some very uncomfortable questions about how one came into possession of an ancient alien tome.

"Okay, so you can't have it checked out scientifically, but surely you read it."

"We would have," Jack said. "But we couldn't. It was written using the same symbols on your amulet. We've never been able to translate it."

Holy cannoli. The book was written in ancient Atlantean. Important was an understatement. The book went far beyond priceless. No wonder somebody wanted it.

"Okay, we need to talk to your predecessor, JP. As soon as possible." I stared at JP, almost daring him to fight me on this. He didn't. He nodded almost meekly. "What does this thing look like?"

Jack gave me one of his quirky half smiles. "That I can help with. It's small. Maybe six inches by four inches." He held his hands up to indicate the size. "About fifty or sixty pages. Handwritten. The cover is a plain brown and looks almost like leather, but isn't. And there's a symbol engraved on the front."

"What's the symbol? Atlantean, I assume."

"No, actually. It's the Heart of Atlantis," Jack said, nodding at the amulet that hung around my neck. "It's in a slightly darker brown than the cover color with blue in the center, same as the stone in the real amulet. Superimposed over that is the image of an object that looks very much like a key."

"Oh, my." I stared at him in shock as Cordelia's words tumbled over and over in my mind.

Find the key to the key.

Chapter 25

"You know where this retired priest lives?" I asked Jack as we climbed back in the car. I pulled my seatbelt across and snapped it in. "It's somewhere in Paris, right?" JP had claimed not to know, which I thought was odd. Then again, I thought the whole damn thing was odd.

"Yeah." Jack was too casual, too nonchalant. And the expression on his face was too uncomfortable. He was hiding something. As usual.

I narrowed my eyes. "Uh huh."

"Look, he's a friend, all right?"

I tried to raise one eyebrow, but gave up and raised both of them. "Why is this such a big deal, Jack?"

He shrugged. "It's not." A slight flush stained his high cheekbones.

"Holy crap, you're embarrassed." I couldn't resist poking at him. "What have you got to be so embarrassed about?"

"It's nothing, okay? We worked together for decades keeping that book safe. I owe him a lot." His knuckles were white on the steering wheel. "I couldn't just let him rot in some care home."

Like the one we'd visited back home in Oregon. Jack didn't need to say it; it was written all over his face. I decided to give him a break.

"So what did you do?"

He started the car, fiddling a little with the heating so he didn't have to look at me. "I have a small apartment in Paris. I let him stay there."

I'm no idiot. There was more to it than that, but I let it go for the moment. I'd find out soon enough. I changed the subject as he pulled back out onto the B road that led out of town.

"This book. You brought it with you when you fled the massacre?"

"Yes. It was one of the things our leader sent with me." He stopped at a four-way stop before turning onto the highway-like A road which led to the freeway. It was a little over two hours to Paris. "We had no idea what it was or what it meant, but we knew it was important in the same way the amulet was important. We couldn't let it be destroyed."

I tucked my hands under my thighs, pressing the palms against the leather seats. It was an odd habit I sometimes had when I wasn't driving. I found it comfortable. Or maybe it was just a way to keep myself from grabbing the steering wheel. Control issues? Me? "Why didn't you take it out of France with you? You got the Heart out without a problem."

Jack shrugged. "Figured it wasn't a good idea to keep both objects together. Just in case. The priest of this village was a friend to the Templars, so it was safe enough here."

Until now. It hung there between us.

"And Sunwalkers? Was the priest a friend to them, too?" I asked.

He glanced at me, face expressionless. He'd noticed I didn't say 'us.' He knew I wouldn't. He might think I was a Sunwalker, but I wasn't ready to go that far. Not until I was sure. The thought of possibly living forever, gaining power from the sun; freaky as hell.

"Yeah. The chapel was already there, along with the hiding place. We just made use of it."

"And over the years, each successive priest has continued the role of protector," I surmised.

"Exactly."

"What about photographs?" I asked. "Didn't anyone ever take pictures? Send them to code breakers or something?"

"Are you nuts?" Jack's tone made it clear he thought I was a moron. "We couldn't let whatever information is in those books out there in public. The risk was too great. We couldn't let any copies be made of the book. We hoped that one day, we'd figure out how to read it. Find out what it was for." He shook his head. "That day still hasn't come, and unless we find the book, it never will."

Except he was only partially right. Maybe we couldn't read the book yet, but I knew what the book was for. If Cordelia and her otherworldly contacts were to be believed, it was the key.

And I was the lock.

***

Jack's "small apartment" in Paris just happened to be a penthouse in one of the gorgeous old buildings on the Île de la Cité in the middle of the Seine. The views of Notre Dame Cathedral and the river were breathtaking. And that was an understatement.

I felt like a kid with her nose pressed up against the glass of a department store, drooling over the latest toy. Only I was drooling over the wonders of Paris. The apartment must have cost a freaking fortune.

A boat slid past on the river, lights strung across its deck, creating magic for the diners enjoying their meal onboard, along with the view. The faint melodies of a string quartet drifted on the breeze. I could imagine myself down there with Jack, sipping wine...Inigo. I'd meant I could imagine myself down there with Inigo. What the hell was my problem?

"If you're done acting like a tourist, Father Nicolas is ready to see us." Jack's voice was dry, as if he'd somehow read my mind.

I turned around and made a face at him to hide the confusion in my heart. "If I want to act like a tourist, I damn well can." I knew it was a childish comeback, but it was the best I had with my head such a mess. Besides which, Paris was beautiful, and I'd never ever had the chance to enjoy such a view from such a place. Probably wouldn't again, either. Even my generous salary didn't run to penthouse apartments in the heart of the City of Lights. "Still, duty calls, I suppose. Lead on." I gave Jack a nod and followed him into the other room.

If I'd thought the view from the living room was magnificent, it was nothing compared to the view from Father Nicolas's bedroom. The intricate stonework of the Cathedral was softened by spring foliage from dozens of shade trees, set against the backdrop of the river sparkling in the early evening sun.

"Breathtaking, isn't it?" The creaky voice caught my attention.

Father Nicolas lay on a hospital bed facing the bank of windows, propped up slightly so he could enjoy the view. His frail body was hooked up to half a dozen beeping machines. He looked about a thousand years old, withered and shrunken, but his eyes shone bright with intelligence. His body may have been wasted, but his mind was sharp.

"Yes," I said with a smile. "It's one of the most amazing things I've ever seen."

"Imagine what heaven will be like."

I didn't bother telling him I didn't believe in heaven. Most religious folk didn't understand my feelings on spirituality and the afterlife, but it was hard to believe the dogma when you'd seen what I had.

"Ah," Father Nicolas said, reading my face as clearly as if I'd spoken. "You don't believe in the afterlife."

"Oh, but I do," I assured him with a smile. "Just not the Christian version."

His eyes twinkled as he folded his hands, spotted and lined with age, calmly in his lap. "Who said I was talking about the Christian version?"

He had me there. I guessed I wasn't the only one who'd seen the world as most people never had. "*Touché*," I said with a laugh. Plopping into a chair next to the bed, I switched subjects. "Jack told you about what happened?" I glanced up at Jack, leaning against the wall next to the headboard. He'd gone into strong-and-silent mode again.

"Yes." Father Nicolas's expression darkened. "It concerns me greatly. I have been lying here thinking who else could know about the book and its hiding place besides Jack, Jean-Pierre, and myself. None of us are the type to share our secrets easily."

I glanced over at Jack again. "No sh...kidding."

Father Nicolas let out a chuckle. I hadn't fooled him one bit.

"Come to any conclusions?" I asked.

"One," he said grimly, the amusement fading from his face.

Jack and I exchanged looks. I had a bad feeling about this. "Sounds like a story," I prompted the old man.

"Yes, and a disturbing one." Father Nicolas's fingers plucked at the coverlet across his lap. "Many years ago, when I was still the caretaker of our lovely little chapel, I met a young man who was visiting France to study the history of the Knights Templar. He asked to meet with me and I agreed. We spoke at some length about various things. He had some...unusual theories."

"What kind of theories?" Jack asked.

Father Nicolas glanced up at him. "The kind of theories that involve magic not of this world."

"Atlantis," I whispered. Somebody had made the connection.

"Yes," Father Nicolas said. "I believe so, though he did not say it outright."

"Who was he?" Jack asked.

"I do not know," the priest admitted. "He gave me a name that was clearly not his own. I believed he was simply trying to keep things on, how do you young people say it? The low down?"

I grinned, despite myself. "The down low."

"Yes. That. Despite my training, I did not see through the man's guise until after I'd shared a few tidbits of information with him." Nicolas held up his hand to forestall Jack's protest. "Nothing of import, mind you. Nothing about the book or the chapel or even about you, but enough to send him in the right direction. There seemed little harm back then, but now I know it was a mistake. Especially when I discovered who the man became." With shaking fingers Nicolas reached for something on the table beside his bed. He handed me an old newspaper clipping.

The lettering was in French, so I couldn't read it, and the ink had faded with time. But what I saw made my heart beat a little faster. I held it up to better catch the light, to make sure, but there was no mistaking the man in the picture. The man who had become Public Enemy Number One: Alister Jones.

Chapter 26

Father Nicolas insisted Alister had never returned to visit him, and the book had never been mentioned during their conversation all those years ago. But somebody had managed to discover its location, and there was no doubt in my mind that somebody was Alister Jones. Still, I couldn't wrap my head around the fact that Jones had, with such limited information, managed to discover the location of the book. My guess was he'd come across something recently to point him in the right direction; otherwise he'd have stolen it decades ago.

"Now what?" I asked Jack as he softly closed the door to Father Nicolas's room behind us.

Before Jack could answer, Father Nicolas's nurse appeared from somewhere within the depths of the apartment. The kitchen, no doubt, since she was carrying a tray with a cup of tea and a bowl of what smelled like split pea soup. I love split pea soup, especially when generously dosed with chunks of ham.

Jack stopped the woman, rattling off a string of French. Since my language skills only went so far as to ask for the bathroom and order wine, I stepped back and let him do his thing. A quick back and forth between the two, and she was on her way to serve Father Nicolas his lunch.

"Okay, what was that about?"

Jack led the way toward the front door. "I asked her if anyone had been to visit in recent weeks."

"Good idea. What did she say?" I pulled the door open, and we started down the steps. There was an elevator, but it was a little sketchy, and I was leery of getting caught in it, what with the whole claustrophobia issue. Besides, a little cardio never hurt anyone.

"She hasn't seen anyone other than the usual church visitors, but she gave me the phone number and address of the night nurse," Jack said. "I think we should pay her a visit. She's more likely to cooperate face-to-face. It's possible someone visited in the evening."

I nodded. It made sense. Come in the evening when the old man was tired and vulnerable. Coerce the information out of him.

I pushed through the main door and out onto the street. I could hear the faint strains of an accordion playing "La Vie En Rose" as a couple of teenagers strolled by licking ice cream cones from Berthillon. I waited as Jack carefully shut the front door behind us.

"Wouldn't Father Nicolas have told us if he'd had a visitor?" I asked. "He didn't seem like the kind of person to lie about something like that."

"He wouldn't lie," Jack said. "Not to me. But it's possible he didn't remember."

I shook my head. "I don't think he's got dementia, Jack. He was in control of his faculties our entire visit."

"Oh, he's sharp as a tack," Jack agreed, "but you and I both know memories can be meddled with."

I gave him a look. "That means JP's memories could have been messed with, too."

His face turned hard. "It's possible," he admitted, "but we need to find out more."

"I agree. Let's go talk to the nurse."

***

Jack and I decided to check into our hotel before speaking to the night nurse. The hotel was only a few streets away, and I felt the need to take a breather. Plus I wanted to call Drago and check on Inigo.

The hotel was what they call "boutique," which, as far as I could see, meant cramped as hell with rude staff and the world's smallest elevator. I did think it was a bit ironic that while Jack owned an enormous penthouse apartment in the heart of Paris, we were stuck in hotel rooms the size of postage stamps.

I tossed my overnight bag on the the floor next to the bed before pulling out my cellphone. Sinking down onto the hard mattress, I rang the number to Drago's private line, the one he kept for close friends and family.

He picked up on the fourth ring. "Morgan, how are you?"

It always startled me when people did that. My brain went to "psychic" before it went to "caller ID." What could I say? I'm programmed for the weird and wonderful. "I'm fine, Drago, just...busy. Got a case."

"Oh, yeah? More murder and mayhem?"

"Something like that." I took a deep breath, bracing myself for the next question. "How is he?"

"Same."

Hot tears burned at the back of my eyes. "Okay. Thanks."

"I'm sorry, little one." His voice was a soothing rumble in my ear. "I wish I could give you more hope, but these things take time."

"Yeah, I know. I just miss him." I couldn't help the little sob that spilled out at the end because I'd heard what he didn't say: that even time might not fix this.

"I know you do, little one." Drago's voice was unusually gentle, as if he thought I might break. He cleared his throat. "You know no one would blame you if you moved on. Not even him. He'd want you to be happy. Have a real life."

"Yeah, thanks. I'll call you in a couple days to check on him. Bye, Drago." I hung up before he could say anything else. I swallowed hard and shoved my phone into my pocket. I would not cry. I wouldn't.

"What did Drago have to say?"

I glanced up, startled. I'd left the door unlocked, and Jack had invited himself in. "How long have you been standing there?"

"Long enough. How are things in the Highlands?"

I shrugged, pulling out my phone to fiddle with it. I didn't want to look at him. "Same."

Jack sank down on the bed next to me. He reached over and took my hand. I stared down at our entwined fingers. His hand was warm and sent delicious tingles up my spine, but it also made me sad and a little pissed off.

"I know you don't want to hear this, Morgan, but I think it's time you moved on."

I yanked my hand away. "What? And come running to you?" I spat out.

"You heard what Drago said. He won't come out of that coma for decades. Maybe even centuries. If he even survives."

It didn't escape my notice that Jack hadn't agreed with me or even acknowledged my comment about him. Typical. He wanted me to be free from other men, but he didn't want to commit to me himself.

"I could still be alive in a century. You said I was a Sunwalker." For the first time since this whole Atlantis thing started, I wanted it to be so. I wanted to be different, other, immortal.

Jack touched my cheek. "Maybe. Maybe not. But even if you do live forever, how long are you willing to wait for a dead man?"

I swallowed hard. Jack was right. And yet, he was so wrong. This was it. The moment where I had to make my choice. I scooted back out of reach, shaking my head slightly. "This is why we'll never work, Jack."

"What do you mean?"

"Everything always has to be your way, in your time. You want me, but only on your terms. I'm just supposed to drop everything and come running."

A muscle flexed in his jaw. I'd definitely hit the mark. "That's not true."

But I could tell from his tone he knew it was true. It was the curse of the alpha male. It was why in real life, real relationships, alpha males rarely worked. Not unless the woman was willing to give up her very essence for him. That wasn't me. I wanted a partner, not a boss.

"I'm sorry, Jack," I stood up and headed for the door. "But this, between us? It's got to stop. No more flirting. No more teasing. No more you want me, and then you don't. I want to be with someone who loves me and wants me all the time. Not just when it's convenient."

***

Father Nicolas's night nurse, Genevieve Collett, lived in a tiny studio apartment way out in the Eighteenth Arrondissement, an area famous for such historical places as the Sacre Coeur and Monmartre. Genevieve, however, lived in the working class neighborhood of Goutte d'Or, where tourists and their rich pockets were few and far between. Probably why she'd chosen it. She could actually afford the rent.

Jack led the way through the crowded, narrow streets. The trip over had been what one could call awkward. Outwardly, he was calm, but inwardly I sensed his seething rage. Under that, there might even have been hurt.

I felt completely calm, almost Zen-like. I'd made my choice, and it was the right one. Inigo was mine. Always. As I was his. And if I had to wait a century, well, Jack had better be right about my Sunwalker status, otherwise Inigo was going to have to get used to having a ghost for a girlfriend.

My mouth watered from the spicy scents emanating from copious North African restaurants as we moved through the streets. My stomach growled. I wondered if I could convince Jack to stop at one of them for lunch after our meeting with Genevieve.

Ducking into one of the many old apartment buildings, we hiked up to the third floor. High enough to be relatively safe and to get a fair amount of exercise, not high enough for exorbitant rent. Smart.

I knocked on the door, standing so the person on the other side of the peephole would be sure to see me, not Jack. I could look innocent and non-threatening when I wanted to.

"*Un moment s'il vous plaît.*" The voice from the other side of the door was muffled but distinctly feminine.

There was the scrape of a bolt from the other side. The door slowly swung open, revealing a chain still firmly in place. A sleepy brown eye appeared in the narrow gap between the door and the frame.

"*Oui?*"

"Genevieve Collett?"

"*Oui.*"

"My name is Morgan Bailey. I'm a friend of Father Nicolas's."

No answer, just confusion in that brown eye. I winced. She probably didn't speak English. I tried again, stumbling over the unfamiliar French words.

"*Mon ami* Father Nicolas." Crap. That wasn't right. "Jack. Do your thing."

Jack stepped into view, which caused Genevieve's visible eye to widen. I wasn't sure if it was in fear or lust. I was going with the latter. Jack was insanely good looking in a rugged, former Templar kind of way. Definitely the type that made women swoon. I should know.

Jack cleared his throat, then let out a string of French. After a pause, Genevieve rattled some words back, and then quietly closed the door. I glanced at Jack.

"She's letting us in," he said. His expression was stoic, and he didn't quite meet my eyes.

I nodded. "I take it she doesn't understand English."

"Not a word."

I sighed. Figured.

The chain rattled and the door swung open, revealing a dainty woman with dusky skin, dark hair, and equally dark eyes. She was exotically pretty in her simple, white cotton robe and bare feet, naturally curly hair sexily tousled from sleep. I felt an irrational stab of jealousy. I never looked that good just out of bed. Mostly, I looked like somebody had whacked me in the head with a two-by-four before letting a wolverine loose on my head.

Genevieve said something in French that was clearly a welcome and waved us to a rust-colored couch. As we sat, I caught a glimpse of an unmade bed behind a Japanese screen. I felt sort of bad waking her up, but we needed information.

She offered us coffee, which we politely refused, before settling into a chair opposite us. Pulling a cobalt blue afghan over her lap, she and Jack got down to business. I sat there feeling dumb. I really should have learned some foreign language or other, but it honestly wasn't my strong suit. I knew every word to *Guantanamera* by heart, but damned if I could speak Spanish to save my life. It went in one ear and out the other without sticking, no matter how hard I tried.

"This is interesting," Jack said, interrupting my train of thought. "She says there was a man that came to visit Father Nicolas a few nights ago. She didn't want to let him in, but he claimed it was an emergency, that he needed to speak with the Father about Jean-Pierre."

"JP? Why didn't Father Nicolas tell us about this?" It seemed weird he'd leave that out.

"She says when the man left, Father Nicolas seemed fine, but he was very tired and went to sleep almost immediately. He didn't tell her what the emergency was, and he was still asleep when she left in the morning. The next evening, when she mentioned the visitor, Father Nicolas claimed not to remember."

I frowned. I could understand the priest not telling his nurse about the visitor's mission, but I was certain he would have told us about it, what with the book and everything. "Double check with her about Father Nicolas's faculties. I want to make sure this isn't dementia." Not that I believed it was for a second.

Jack asked Genevieve a question. She shook her head emphatically, dark eyes wide, a rush of words spilling from her.

"She says he's as rational as you or I. She says him forgetting any conversation was very odd, and it has troubled her, but she didn't know what to do about it. The day nurse just laughed it off as old age."

I mulled it over. "The more I think about it, the more I'm convinced someone managed to manipulate the Father somehow. Caused him to forget the visit and whatever it was they discussed. Maybe even forced him to reveal secrets without realizing it."

Jack shrugged. "Anything is possible, and I'd say that's very high on the list of possibilities."

He was right about that. This whole thing just smelled rotten. "Can you ask her to describe the man?"

He turned back to Genevieve and asked the question. She nodded eagerly, rattling off another string of words before hopping off the chair and rushing behind the Japanese screen.

"She says she can do better. She took a picture of him when he wasn't looking."

"Clever girl."

Genevieve reappeared, cellphone in hand. She handed it to Jack. One look and his eyes went wide. He quickly passed the phone to me.

I had half-expected the picture to be of Alister Jones, but it wasn't. It was Brent Darroch.

Chapter 27

I don't know why I was surprised to discover the man who had visited Father Nicolas was my nemesis, Brent Daroch. We'd known, or at least suspected, for some time that Alister and Darroch were working together. What we didn't know was why.

I ran my hand along the cool wood of the bannister as Jack and I descended the steps from Genevieve's third floor walkup. Our footsteps echoed loud in the stairwell. For all the noise on the street, Genevieve's building was surprisingly quiet. It gave me a moment to mull over the Darroch revelation.

There was something else that niggled at me.

"How on earth did Brent Darroch get Father Nicolas to spill his secrets in the first place?" I wondered aloud as I jogged down the stairs behind Jack. "And how did he remove the memories without help?" I was pretty sure Genevieve would have mentioned the Fairy Queen if she'd shown up at the door. She was kind of hard to forget. "It's impossible. Brent may have Atlantean blood, but he hasn't got the power." Which was why he'd wanted the Heart of Atlantis in the first place. So he wouldn't have to team up with anyone else.

"No idea," Jack said.

Fat lot of help he was. "Okay, so why didn't Alister get the information? He's far more powerful than Darroch." Not in a superpower way, but in a convincing sort of way. "And he'd met Father Nicolas before. Wouldn't it be easier to waltz in and take up where they left off?"

Jack stopped so abruptly, I nearly ran into his back. "Maybe that's it."

"What's it?"

He turned toward me. "Maybe whatever Darroch did to Father Nicolas only worked because they didn't know each other. Maybe if Alister had tried it, it wouldn't have worked."

I mulled that over as we continued down the steps. "Okay, so like whatever they do scrapes off the top memories because they're recent. But the memory of meeting Alister would have been implanted much deeper, since it was years ago. No way to erase it."

"Something like that."

It sort of made sense, though it didn't explain how Darroch had managed to mess with the priest's mind without the Fairy Queen in tow. A thought struck me as we reached the bottom of the steps. "Holy crap."

"What?"

"Come on." I grabbed Jack by the arm and pulled him out into the street. "I'm hungry. Let's get some lunch, and I'll tell you what I think."

***

Jack stared at me as if I'd suddenly grown a second head. "You seriously think the Fairy Queen is behind all this?"

"Not exactly." I stuffed another chunk of bread in my mouth, followed by a healthy spoonful of *tagine*. Yummy. The spicy lamb dish was perfect. I swallowed. "The Fairy Queen has the ability to erase memories and replace them with something. New ones, I imagine. She must have lent that power to Darroch somehow. Temporarily, at least."

"Can she do that?"

I shrugged. "Why not? She's got abilities far beyond anything I've ever seen."

"Why, then? What's in it for her?"

I shrugged. "Dunno. But whatever it is, right now I'm betting her goals coincide with Alister's. And Darroch is either a full partner or along for the ride, playing his own angle." I was betting on the latter. Darroch always had his own angle.

"And the Queen is willing to work with them." Jack sounded doubtful, but I was convinced we were on the right track.

"For now. For a price." I took another big bite of *tagine*. Gods, I couldn't get enough of the stuff.

"And you think Alister is willing to pay that price?" he asked with one eyebrow raised.

"I think Alister is willing to pay almost any price for power." I swirled the bread through the *tagine* sauces and popped it in my mouth. "I also think Alister is arrogant enough to believe he can outsmart the Queen of the Sidhe. I bet he figures he won't have to pay the price. That he'll come out on top." That was Alister all over.

"That, we can agree on." Jack took a bite of his *tagine*. "This brings me back."

I knew what he was talking about: the Crusades. He must have eaten similar food while he was in the Holy Lands. He didn't talk about it much, and being something of a history nerd, I was eager to hear more. "How long were you there?"

A pause. "Long enough." His expression closed as he glanced away from me.

Okay then. I know when I'm not wanted. This was another reason why Jack and I hadn't worked. He would never let me in. Inigo, on the other hand, had welcomed me in with open arms. I was always the one holding back. The stab of pain that accompanied that thought took my breath away. I shoved aside thoughts of Inigo. I needed to focus on the business at hand. Thinking of him would only make it an impossible task.

"We need to figure out what it is both Alister and the Queen want. Wait, duh." I practically smacked myself in the forehead. "We know what they want. They were after the book and they got it. But why? What do they want with it?" Other than to control me and whatever I was supposed to be able to do as the Key of Atlantis. I mean, there had to be a reason, some end game.

"I wish I knew," Jack said. "But like I told you before, we never knew what was in the book."

I thought it over as I finished off the last of my *tagine* and flat bread. "Maybe they figured out how to translate it?"

"How? Alister doesn't speak or read ancient Atlantean. No one does."

"Darroch can. He figured out the ancient prophecy." I didn't bother to remind Jack the prophecy was supposedly about me.

Jack shook his head as he stood up, throwing a wad of green and red euros on the table. "Not well enough, and not without help from your amulet. Darroch probably got most of his knowledge from the dreams and from gossip. Now that you wear the amulet, he's cut off from the dreams."

I followed him out the door onto the busy street. All around me, people shouted in French and other exotic languages I didn't recognize. Dark eyes stared at me from every direction, some with appreciation and some with suspicion. This part of Paris was heavily North African, and I stuck out like the proverbial sore thumb. Ignoring the stares, I focused on Jack and our conversation.

"Then it has to be the Queen, right?" Things were clicking for me now. "After all, the Sidhe were still here in this realm when the Atlanteans arrived. Maybe they learned enough before they crossed to the Other World to translate the book."

Jack frowned as he thought it over. "It's possible." He didn't sound convinced.

"It's more than possible," I insisted. "It totally makes sense. There's something in that book both Alister and the Fairy Queen want so much they're working together. Alister to obtain the book, and Morgana to translate."

"But you're forgetting one thing."

I glanced up at him. "What's that?"

"There's no way they could have known what was in the book prior to stealing it. How would they know it would be useful?"

"Maybe you're right," I admitted. "Or maybe they did know somehow. After all, Darroch found out about the amulet. Maybe there was more he didn't tell us." In fact, it was damn likely. "Or maybe the Sidhe knew about it from back in the day."

"It doesn't matter either way. This is all speculation." There was anger in Jack's tone, though his face bore its usual stoic expression. "For whatever reason, they have the book now, and we have no idea where they are."

"True," I admitted. "But we have a secret weapon."

"What's that?" Another raised eyebrow.

"Eddie. Let's head back to the hotel. I feel the need to Skype."

Chapter 28

Eddie's cherubic face came into view on my laptop screen, or at least the bottom half of his face did. I could count his nose hairs.

"Uh, Eddie," I said, "I think you need to back away from the computer just a bit."

"Oh, dear. Just a moment."

I repressed a giggle as I settled against the headboard. Jack didn't even crack a smile. In fact, he looked downright sullen, lounging against the door of my hotel room. I turned back to the screen, determined to ignore his royal sulkiness.

Over the laptop speakers I heard a bit of shuffling, followed by a loud *thunk*. Finally, the whole of Eddie's face came into view, beaming from ear to ear. "How's this?"

"Much better." I didn't bother to tell him he didn't need to speak quite so loud. I just turned down the volume.

"Excellent." Eddie leaned back on his stool and I could see he was sitting at the counter of Majicks and Potions, his little New Age book and gift shop. He was wearing a fuchsia waistcoat over a mustard colored button-down shirt. It was an eye popping combination, to say the least. "I'm still trying to get used to this whole video chatting thing. It's so Star Trek." He practically beamed with excitement.

"How are you, Eddie? How's everything in Portland?"

"Oh, wonderful. Wonderful. It's raining, as usual. But not to worry, I'm packing for a steampunk cruise. Seven days of Caribbean sun, corsets, and bowler hats. Not to mention the food! But I digress.

How is Paris? I remember a time back in the eighties..."

"Yeah, Paris is great," I interrupted. I so did not want to hear stories of Eddie in the eighties. My imagination was bad enough. "Really beautiful."

"Did you get a chance to visit Notre Dame? It really is a must-see. The stained glass and statuary are truly stunning."

"Uh, no. We haven't had time yet."

"Of course, of course. You're there on business." Eddie adjusted his little round spectacles. "I'm sure you didn't call just to chat about the wonders of the City of Lights. How can I help you?"

I gave him a quick run-down on Darroch's escape, soul vamps, Alister's involvement, and the theft of the mysterious book. "Frankly, we're at an impasse. We don't know what the book is for, and we've no idea where to find it. Alister and Darroch have gone completely off the grid, as far as we can tell."

"Hmmmm." Eddie pulled on his lower lip, his eyes taking on a faraway look. I was about to say something when he finally jarred himself out of whatever rabbit hole he'd fallen down. "Yes, yes. I think I recall something of this book."

"Really?" I turned my head slightly and shot Jack a glare. "Jack says nobody knew about it but the Templars and their allies."

"No, no. I'm sure there's something..." Eddie trailed off as he moved out of frame, leaving me staring at the blank wall. There was a lot of rustling off camera, followed by a heavy *thump* and some more muttering. Then Eddie reappeared, waving what looked like a cheap paperback novel from the sixties.

"*Footprints of the Gods*," he said, flipping through the pages. "I know some people think it's right up there with Ancient Astronaut theory, but we all know just how not crazy that is, don't we?" He waggled his eyebrows while giving me a meaningful look.

I knew he was referring to the fact that the ancient Atlanteans had come from another planet thousands of years ago, and their blood flowed in my veins. Not just in mine, either, but a lot of people's. Mainstream scientists could mock all they wanted. Some of the craziest theories about human ancestry weren't that far from the truth.

"How is that," I pointed to the paperback with its lurid orange lettering and classic flying saucer, "going to help us find the book we're looking for?"

"Find it?" Eddie peered at me through his little round spectacles. "Oh, no, it won't do that, but it might tell us what is so important about it, and how Alister Jones discovered it in the first place. And that, my dear Morgan, may help us discover where it is now."

I still couldn't see how a dusty old paperback from five decades ago was going to do that, but whatever. Eddie had a way of uncovering the most interesting bits of information from the most random places. I fidgeted a little as he slowly scanned a few pages. Jack stood unmoving against the closed door, carefully avoiding my gaze.

"Ah," Eddie exclaimed, "here it is. Let's see. Interesting."

"What is it, Eddie?" I prodded.

"Oh, yes, sorry. According to this, there were stories of a book found in the Holy Land."

"Let me guess," I said. "By the Templars."

"Why, yes." Eddie beamed at me before returning to the paperback.

When Jack first told me the story of discovering the cave under the Mount, he hadn't mentioned finding the book, along with the amulet and the dead Atlanteans. Granted, he had a way of leaving things out. Important things.

"Jack told me they found it with some bodies, and the Heart of Atlantis."

"The author is not so specific, but it says here the book was rumored to be made of a mysteriously indestructible material. The pages contained indecipherable symbols. Some people believed they were a message from the gods themselves."

"Sounds like the right book. Any idea what this message said?"

Eddie frowned, flipping through a few more pages. "The author naturally postulates the book was written by an ancient alien explorer. A journal, perhaps, of his adventures. Possibly information regarding his advanced civilization."

"Wow, he was right on the money," I said dryly. We knew without a doubt the book was Atlantean. We just didn't know what was in it, and Eddie's little paperback wasn't helping.

"He also speculates the book was the treasure the Templars took back with them to France from the Holy Land."

I sighed. "Part of it, anyway."

"Indeed." Eddie nodded. "He also claims they kept the book carefully hidden in one of their secret locations, guarded night and day."

"That explains how Alister knew to start looking in Templar chapels. No doubt it was his best lead." And it had proved dead on. "How the hell did some fringe scientist from way back when figure all this stuff out?"

Eddie glanced up from the book. "Secrets sometimes have a way of slipping out no matter how carefully they are guarded."

"So, nothing more on the book itself, huh?"

"Unfortunately not. My guess," Eddie said, putting aside the paperback, "is the book is much more than a simple diary."

"No shit."

He ignored my language. "Since Darroch and Jones want it so badly, it must contain something they want."

I refrained from pointing out he was stating the obvious. "Right. And what they want is the power of the amulet. But it's too late. It's already chosen me." Not that I was entirely happy about it, but at least it was staying out of Alister's clutches. If only I could figure out his end game. I mean, besides the power grab.

"Is it? Too late, I mean." Eddie took off his glasses, polished them with a hot pink handkerchief, and shoved them back on his face. "The amulet chose you, certainly. But if that were the end of it, why would Alister be trying so very hard to get his hands on it?"

Eddie made a good point, and a very uncomfortable one. "You think there is a way he can still get his hands on the power?"

"Yes. Yes, I do. And I also believe this book he's taken is the key to doing just that."

"Freaking fantastic."

***

"How does this help us?" Jack snapped after I'd signed off with Eddie. "We already know whatever is in the book is important. What we need to know is where it is and how to get it back."

"We know where it is," I snarled back, at my wit's end with his bad attitude. "Alister has it."

"We don't know that. We're guessing. And we'd already guessed it before we talked to Eddie. We're no closer to understanding it than we were before. We still don't know *where* Alister is, and we still don't know what the book says. Only the rambling suppositions of some crazy old man."

If I hadn't already been in full blown pissed-off mode, that snark against Eddie would have done it. Without another word, I grabbed my jacket and stormed out of the hotel room, leaving Jack behind yelling about immaturity or some bullshit. Frankly, I didn't give a damn. Eddie had done his best. Maybe we didn't know anything more than what we'd already guessed, other than where Alister had probably gotten his information on the book. But Eddie's speculations confirmed my own, and it was the best we could do for now.

I took the stairs, needing the exercise. Also, because I had no intention of getting on the tiny little excuse for an elevator in our Parisian hotel. I'd rather not deal with a full blown panic attack from claustrophobia.

The lobby was overcrowded with people checking in and out, and hotel employees running to and fro. Piles of luggage created an obstacle course to the front door. Swinging on my jacket, I strode toward the glass doors, ignoring the glares from tourists who clearly thought my single-minded bid for freedom was rude in the extreme. Frankly, I thought it was rude they weren't watching where they were going.

The fresh air hit me, and I filled my lungs, dragging in the scents of Paris in the springtime. Actually, it didn't smell that much different from Portland unless one counted the *boulangerie* a few doors down. Whatever they were baking smelled like nirvana.

Ignoring the siren's song of baked goods, I crossed the street and headed roughly in the direction of the River Seine. It was getting on toward sunset and the weather was decent; the wide walkways on either side of the river thick with Parisians and tourists all taking in the evening air.

I leaned against the railing of the Pont Saint-Louis, staring down at the river as it flowed beneath me, trying to calm my mind. For the first time since we'd arrived in France, I allowed the focus on our mission to drop away and truly enjoyed the moment. I didn't know what it was about this place, but every time I visited Paris, at some point in the trip, I found my way to this exact spot. And every time I did, something about it would suck me into the poetry and beauty of the City of Lights. Everything else would melt away and I would just...be.

I closed my eyes and inhaled deeply, curling my fingers around the cold metal railing. A cool breeze toyed with my hair. The murmur of something said in French caressed my ears. More than two thousand years of history, of life, of love sank into my bones.

Opening my eyes, I turned around so I could take in the gothic beauty of Notre Dame Cathedral. Softened by blooming trees and the blaze of the setting sun, the ancient church was like something out of a fairy tale.

I let my gaze roam over the passing humanity: a loving couple holding hands and whispering romantic things while stealing kisses; a family of four bickering about where to eat; a trio of Japanese girls giggling to each other while snapping photos of everything in sight. Let me rephrase: every cute boy in sight. An elderly man passed, sucking on a pipe walking his tiny dog.

I rubbed my temple as a sudden tightness clenched at my skull. And then I saw him on the other side of the Quai aux Fleurs. Just a shadow among other shadows, but his eyes glowed an eerie red as he stared directly at me. My fingers tightened on the railing behind me as my entire body froze. A soul-imbued vampire, here in Paris.

Our eyes locked, and he knew I'd seen him. Between one heartbeat and the next, he took off running, straight up the Quai du Marché-Neuf toward the Notre Dame Cathedral with me hot on his heels.

Chapter 29

The vampire moved with incredible speed. His feet flew over the paving stones in a dizzying blur, shoving gawking tourists out of his way. If his eyes hadn't already given away his nature, his attempt at escape would have. It wasn't the first time I'd seen a red-eyed vampire outside the city of Portland, and I wasn't about to let the bastard get away.

A woman screamed, tumbling to the ground as the vampire pushed her down before vanishing into the crowd. I would have stopped, but fortunately there were plenty of helping hands, and the woman appeared more rattled than hurt. Instead I shouted, "Which way?"

An older gentleman with a huge camera around his neck waved his hand. "That way. Get the bastard," he yelled in a thick Texas accent.

With a nod, I sped up, searching for my prey. Eventually, I caught sight of him again. I dashed after his retreating form, dodging through the gaps he'd made in the wall of humanity. Hopefully, most people would assume they'd seen two Olympic sprinters out on a practice run. The last thing anyone needed were rumors of vampires loose on the streets of Paris. Not that the locals would be too much in an uproar. In typical Parisian fashion, they'd just shrug and roll with it. It was the tourists who would be a problem.

The vamp sprinted across the street, and I darted after him. Unfortunately, the gap between us was widening. For all my hunter speed and strength, I was no match for him. Maybe he really had been an Olympic sprinter.

Reaching within, I grabbed hold of the Darkness that lived inside me. With barely a pause, it surged up and out. My vision tunneled down to a pinprick as the Darkness pulled strength from the heavy shadows surrounding the Cathedral. It pushed speed into my legs, breath into my lungs. A laugh spilled from my throat and all I could think was *free at last.* The world around me blurred as I picked up speed, my boots striking a staccato rhythm against the paving stones.

The vampire crossed the wide open square in front of the Cathedral. During the day, the area was packed with tourists, but now there were only a few stragglers huddled around the edges. They stared at the two of us as though they'd never seen a high-speed foot chase before. The vampire headed for one of the enormous front doors looming up behind the temporary chain link fence. Surely he knew the Cathedral would be closed at this time of evening?

Either he didn't know or didn't care. He rushed right up to the door, grabbed the handle, and gave it a jerk. It didn't move. He let out a string of cuss words that had even me flinching. Even though I didn't exactly believe in the Christian God, I sort of half-expected the vamp to get struck by lightening for cussing in front of a church.

The vampire glanced back at me, eyes widening as he realized how close I was. My lips curled into one of those scary smiles the Darkness enjoyed showing people it was hunting. Yep, at this point, the Darkness was pretty much in charge. I didn't bother fighting it. I had more important things to focus on.

For a moment, the vampire hesitated. Then, whirling to the right, he scurried around the corner of the hulking stone building and disappeared.

I snarled. Or rather, the Darkness snarled. "Oh, no, you don't."

I dashed around the building in time to see the vamp kick in a smaller side door. There was a sharp *crack,* accompanied by a spray of splinters, and then the vampire slipped inside.

A vampire hiding in a church. Talk about ironic.

I slowed down, much to the dismay of the Darkness, cautiously peering into the dimly lit interior. No telling where the vamp was or what he was planning, but the last thing I needed was him ripping my throat out because I wasn't paying attention.

The Darkness snarled again, impatient. Caution was definitely not in its nature.

"Shut up," I mumbled under my breath. Oh, gods I was talking to myself.

Stepping over the shattered remains of the door, I kept my ears peeled for any sound from within. There was nothing; just the stillness of a building that had expelled its visitors and now sat empty with a sigh of relief. Surely there must still be a few nuns or priests or whatever hanging around, cleaning up, counting the sales of religious trinkets from the booths near the entrance. The doors hadn't closed that long ago.

I listened again. If there was anyone left inside, they were far away from this part of the Cathedral.

I slipped through the narrow hallway, the heavy musk of age and mildew assaulting my nose. I reached out to touch the wall, ground myself in the deep shadows. My fingers slid across cool stone and smooth wood as I made my way into the sanctuary.

Faint light trickled through the stained glass windows, so little as to be nearly useless. The exit signs gave off a faint greenish glow. Again, useless to the normal human eye, but my eyesight quickly adjusted. Between my hunter abilities and the Darkness channeling its way through me, I could see just as clearly as if someone had turned on floodlights.

I turned my head, trying to spot my prey. Narrow wooden pews, dark with age, lined the middle of the enormous open area facing the altar. That was where the priests would say mass or whatever. I'd seen one once, years ago when I'd been just a tourist. I had actually kind of liked the chanting. It had had a soothing quality.

Around the outside of the seating area was a wide avenue lined with velvet rope. It was there that the tourists could wander along, gawking at the goings on in the center of the room and at the carved stone statues of saints lining the walls. My favorite statue was the one of Joan of Arc, and I couldn't help pausing for a second to glance her way.

In the dim light, the white marble shimmered like a ghost. She seemed almost alive, as if she were watching me from her little alcove. Maybe it would have been spooky to someone else, but to me it felt like a benediction. If I had believed in such things.

Behind me, I heard a noise. The scuff of rubber against stone, perhaps. So faint, it almost didn't register.

Instinct and training kicked in, and I dove for the floor just as something whistled through the air where my head had been. I had seconds before my attacker regained his stance. I rolled to the left and under the velvet rope as the weapon clanged against the stone floor with enough force to make me wince. It missed by a hair.

From what I could make out, it was some kind of battle axe, heavy and ancient. Where had he gotten such a thing inside a church? And for that matter, what was with people attacking me with axes lately?

Just like in the Other World with the boar-man, I was on the defensive. I didn't like it. Neither did the Darkness.

I scrambled to the nearest pew, and squeezed under the seat into the next aisle. The axe blade bit into the back of the pew, splintering it in two as I jumped to my feet and ran like hell for the wide open space at the front. A chunk of wood hit me in the cheek, slicing through skin. Hot blood slid over my skin, dripping onto my leather jacket. Wonderful. It would match all the other blood stains.

The scent of my blood enraged the vampire even more. He stormed after me, screaming "Die, bitch!" as he slashed and hacked at empty air, half out of his mind. If he'd been an animal, I'd have said he was rabid.

I nearly stumbled on the stairs up to the altar, mind racing. I had little in the way of conventional weapons at my disposal. A couple knives, and that was it. My main blades and UV gun were back at the hotel. I hadn't exactly been planning on a hunt. Besides, even though I'd been able to bring a weapons stash with me, the French authorities technically didn't allow foreign hunters to carry arms within their borders. We were supposed to call a local hunter to take care of any "unpleasantness" we stumbled into. Sort of hard to do that with a vampire swinging an axe at your head.

I did, however, have one hell of an unconventional arsenal at my disposal.

I hesitated. Every time I let my powers out, it felt like I was walking a fine line between sanity and madness. Only the Darkness seemed marginally controllable these days. Still, I had no choice unless I wanted to become vamp food.

I turned and faced the monster.

Chapter 30

I stood, feet braced, awaiting my attacker. Within my mind, I dove down into the place where my powers lived. The Fire was first, zipping out like it had hit an oil slick, spreading down my arms and across my hands. I could feel it was even in my eyes, a spot of brightness in the middle of a black tunnel of Darkness. The vampire faltered, red eyes panicked.

"Who's the bitch now?" I whispered. Except it wasn't me speaking. The Darkness used my voice.

I wasn't sure the vamp heard me. By that time, the Air was spiraling out of the center of my chest, white smoky mists whipping around like a coiling cobra. My short hair danced wildly on increasingly violent winds. The altar cloth flapped madly, and a vase tipped over, spilling water and day lilies across the apse.

Next came that new power, unfurling almost gently from the deepest part of my being. That iridescent green thing, uncoiling slowly like a seedling sprouting from the earth. My whole body began to take on the faintest green shimmer. Even the fire and the mist had a green tinge.

Below my feet, the stones of the ancient cathedral began to grumble and shake. The building gave a slight heave, sending centuries of dust sprinkling from the ceiling. The chandeliers swayed gently as the ground gave another ominous rumble.

The vampire let out a string of words in French that would have made a sailor blush. And I didn't even speak French.

"*Mon dieu,*" he whispered. "What are you?"

"Your worst nightmare." My lips curved in an ugly smile. The Darkness thrummed with excitement as it watched with my eyes and smiled with my lips. I think the vampire knew it.

Pale fingers released the axe. As it crashed to the floor, the red faded from his eyes, leaving dark wells of nothing. He shook his head as though waking from a long sleep. Something sparked deep in those dead eyes. "Please," was all he said.

I cocked my head to the side. My powers found him a curiosity. But the part of me that was still human found him horrifying. Another soul trapped inside a dead body. Awake. Aware. Dear gods. What kind of monster could do this to another human being?

This had to be stopped. I had to stop it. "Tell me where I can find Alister Jones." My voice was an echoing hollow. Only it wasn't my voice. It was the Darkness.

He opened his mouth, and then shook his head. Stubbornness or fear. I was going with the latter.

"Darroch is no longer controlling you." I knew because the red had gone out of his eyes. I didn't know if he'd fought it off or if something about my powers negated the effects, but the control was gone. "Tell me."

"I don't know." He cast his gaze to the floor. His lie was obvious. I could almost smell it on him. The Darkness snarled in anger.

"Tell me."

The vampire sighed, seeming to fold in on himself. He was older than I'd first thought. A couple hundred years at least. It must be his soul that was young. I shivered, feeling suddenly ill.

"Underground. He's somewhere underground."

I frowned. Jean-Pierre's chapel had an underground. Surely Alister hadn't gone back there. He'd gotten what he wanted. What would be the point?

"Where? Where is this underground?"

"With the bones. He's with the bones." The vampire's voice was faint, like someone half asleep.

"What do you mean? What bones?"

The vamp shook his head. He seemed confused. He opened his mouth, but all that came out was garbled French, none of which I understood. Except for one word: *mort.* Dead.

I reached out to grab his arm. As my fingers touched his skin, the green danced from me to him, wrapping itself around him, winding and twining in a glittery vine. He stared down at the green spreading across his body, up his arm to his shoulder. I imagined my face was a mirror of his: shock, horror, confusion.

And beneath all that, something else. For me, or rather my powers, it was joy. For him, it looked surprisingly like hope.

The green spread across his chest and down his torso, wrapping itself around his thighs. It curled up his throat, dove into his mouth and eyes, and spilled back out his nose. He shimmered with green light, growing brighter and brighter.

Something made me step back. I watched as he spasmed and jerked, choking on the green. In the recesses of my mind, I realized how odd it was.

Vampires didn't need to breathe. I also realized I should be horrified by what was happening, but I wasn't. It was as if I knew deep inside this needed to happen, that it was, somehow, *good.* Once the vampire's body was covered, the green stopped spreading. The vamp stared at me, eyes wide. He tried to speak, but nothing came out past the green.

I don't know what made me say it. The words came unbidden to my lips, as they had once before, but this time they were a soft whisper. A benediction. "Ashes to ashes."

The coils of green suddenly tightened like a snake around its prey. Between one heartbeat and the next, the vampire exploded into so much dust, and I watched a tiny wisp of something like smoke or mist drift away and disappear into the night. A soul returning to the universe.

"Dust to dust."

***

It was full dark by the time I stepped outside again. I tried to ignore the shakiness of my legs as I made my way across the side lawn toward the river. I stuck to the shadows, more comfortable there than in the warm glow of the streetlights. Now that was something to ponder for later.

I stumbled to the rail separating the pedestrian walkway from the sheer drop to the water. Wrapping my fingers around the railing, I held on so hard, my knuckles turned white. It was all that was keeping me on my feet. Once the powers retreated, there wasn't much left in me but sheer exhaustion. I sucked in a deep breath. In through the nose, out through the mouth.

By now, I was shaking, trembling so hard I bit the inside of my cheek until I tasted blood. Over and over, my mind replayed the image of my Earth power squeezing the life, such as it was, out of the vampire.

"You released him," I reminded myself. "You set him free." I knew it without a shadow of a doubt. I'd seen the trapped soul leave. Just like I'd seen Zip's leave her body after the Marid killed her.

It didn't help. I'd killed the vampire with my powers, but that wasn't what bothered me. He'd been a soul trapped inside a virus-ridden corpse. Setting that soul free was right and good. There was no shame in it.

What bothered me was I hadn't cared about his death. I hadn't felt anything.

That was a lie. I'd felt something. I'd felt...glee.

As far as I was concerned, there was a vast difference between the pragmatism of killing monsters for the greater good and killing a creature with a soul, even if it was a trapped soul. Someone else's soul. And there was a huge difference between job satisfaction and actually getting off on the kill.

Tonight, I was afraid I might have finally crossed that line.

Chapter 31

"Are you insane?"

I peered at Jack's reflection in the mirror before returning to the task of cleaning the wound on my cheek. Fortunately, the cut was shallow and the wood chip hadn't left behind any splinters. "Don't be an ass, Jack."

His face turned so red, I thought he might explode. "Going out there," he stabbed one long finger in the general direction of the hotel window, "by yourself was just plain stupid."

I very much wanted to punch him in the face. Instead I said quite calmly, "I'm not a child."

"Only a child would say that."

I whirled to face him, clenching my fists. I wanted to scream in anger. Instead, I kept my voice as calm as I possibly could. "No, only a woman who is being treated like a child by an oversized asshat would say that. I am no helpless female waiting for someone to save her from the bad men. I am a hunter. I am perfectly capable of taking care of myself, and I damn well go where I damn well please." I didn't bother to point out it was his earlier asshattery that had driven me to take to the streets in the first place.

"You're practically unarmed. In a strange place."

I snorted. "I've been to Paris before. And I'm about as unarmed as a porcupine."

That one made him think. He opened his mouth, ready to argue further.

"Enough." A hint of the Darkness leaked into my voice, only partially by accident. It stopped Jack dead. He stared at me as the blood drained from his face. It had been a mean, underhanded thing to do, but I was tired of arguing. Tired of the constant need to prove myself. If I was counting, this was yet another reason why Jack and I would never work. He didn't trust me. Worse, he didn't respect me. Not as a woman, and certainly not as a warrior. I don't know if it was because he came from a different time period or what, but it wasn't something I wanted to live with.

I turned back to the mirror, dismissing the conversation as I dabbed a little beeswax ointment onto the cut. No sense getting an infection even if I was a quick healer. "We have two mysteries to solve. First, we need to find the book."

Jack nodded reluctantly, accepting the subject change. "Which the vampire told you was hidden underground with some bones."

"Yes. If he's talking about JP's little chapel, we're screwed. Alister Jones is definitely not there."

He shook his head. "No bones there. Can't be that."

I tossed the pot of ointment back in my bag. "Okay. Then I'm thinking maybe an ossuary of some kind."

"Catacombs."

"What?"

"Paris has catacombs."

I knew that. Everybody knew that. "So?"

"So, there is a portion of the catacombs where all the bones that were collected from the cemeteries were stored. That's your ossuary."

"Makes sense. I guess city land was too precious to waste on dead people, huh?" I didn't bother hiding the snark.

"Exactly."

"That fits the description. I guess we look there for the book." I had no idea how we were supposed to find one book in a mess of catacombs, if it was even there. I was also getting tired of all this underground nonsense. So not a fan.

"That's settled. The second thing?" Jack asked.

I stared at him for a moment as I wiped my fingers on the cheap hotel towel, my mind still focused on ancient tunnels and old bones. "Oh, right. Second mystery is Brent Darroch's role in this whole thing. How he managed to manipulate someone else's memories. His control over vampires."

"Agreed. Nothing good is bound to come of it."

No shit, Sherlock. I cleared my throat. "Then, of course, there's the issue of stopping Alister and Darroch from their whole world-domination-by-soul-vamp thing. Though that's not really a mystery, per se. We just have to find them and take a sledgehammer to whatever equipment they're using. If the technology is destroyed, they're done." I doubted Alister could rebuild it, seeing as how, in thirty years, the SRA hadn't figured it out.

"As long as they don't have more equipment, or specs hidden elsewhere," Jack pointed out.

Killjoy.

I tossed the towel onto the bathroom counter and stepped back into the bedroom. "Okay, I say we hit the catacombs." It was the best idea I had. Mostly because we had no other leads to go on at the moment.

"Fine. We'll go first thing in the morning."

I gave him a look. "Why wait?"

"It doesn't open until ten."

I smirked. "Since when has that stopped us?"

***

The streets around Notre Dame Cathedral had nearly emptied by the time we crossed the river back into St. Germain on the mainland of Paris. No one paid us any attention, wrapped up in their own little worries and dreams. The cafes, on the other hand, were heaving, golden light spilling out into the streets. Both indoor and outdoor tables were full to overflowing with diners, drinkers, and smokers, everybody yelling in French at top volume. Clouds of cigarette smoke made my eyes burn and my throat tighten. My extrasensory abilities tended to make me more vulnerable to pollutants, not less.

Past the line of cafes, Jack made a sharp turn into an alley off the main thoroughfare. We were still close to the river. I heard the blast from a barge whistle and smelled the damp in the air. The alley ran between two dark shops and dead-ended in a brick wall, a dumpster pushed neatly into the corner. The top of the wall was studded with wrought iron *fleur-de-lis,* a border between the alley and whatever was beyond. They didn't fool me one bit. In the center of each *fleur* was a very nasty looking spike. Trust the French to make home security beautiful and stylish.

"I don't see any entrance here, Jack. Not unless you plan to climb over that wall. If so, you're on your own."

"I like my manhood where it is, thanks. Help me with this." He headed toward the dumpster. With a frown, I followed him.

The dumpster was about half the size of a normal American one, which meant it was average for most of Europe. Judging by the stench, it was also full. Fantastic.

We managed to maneuver the dumpster out of the corner with a great deal of pushing and shoving and only a moderate amount of cussing from me. Jack muttered a lot of stuff in French, so I'm guessing he was being a potty mouth, too. He just sounded more refined than I did.

Once we had the dumpster pushed out of the corner, I realized why we were here. I crouched down for a better look.

"One of these things is not like the other," I said in a light sing-song.

"It's a manhole cover."

"No kidding." I ran my hand over the stone. It was smooth and worn with time. Quite a bit larger than the other paving stones around it, someone had carved drain holes in it the shape of teardrops. The thing was ancient. "How old is it?"

"No idea," he said with a shrug. "It's been here as long as I remember. Maybe even since the Romans."

"How is that possible?" I was a little vague on my history, but I was pretty sure Paris had been rebuilt a time or two since the Roman occupation.

"Back then, they reused everything. It's possible someone found it at some point and decided to put it to good use. What does it matter? It's here now, and this is our way into the catacombs."

"How? It looks pretty well sealed."

"Looks can be deceiving." Jack crouched down on the other side of the stone. "You take that end. And be careful. It's heavy."

"No shit, Sherlock." I stuck my fingers through the teardrop shaped holes. They just fit.

Jack ignored my snarkiness. "Now lift."

I grunted with the effort, my arms shaking a little, but he was right. What had appeared to be grout sealing the stone in place turned out to be a clever camouflage of loose sand and clay. The stone lifted easily from its resting place. Well, as easily as a three-hundred-pound rock could lift, anyway. My back and arms gave a twinge of protest as we hauled it up and out of the hole before sliding it across the paving stones with a screech that made me shudder.

The hole was just wide enough to allow passage of an average-sized man. Unfortunately, Jack was no average-size anything. And I had hips.

I eyeballed the dark hole suspiciously. "Are you sure we're going to fit?"

"Of course. I've done it before."

I glanced up at him, startled. He'd never mentioned that little tidbit before. "When?"

"A long time ago. Now, ladies first?"

"No thanks." No way in hell was I going down there in the dark unknown first. Not with a thousand pounds of dirt between me and the sky. Not to mention, with my luck I'd get wedged in with my ass halfway through. Jack could damn well squeeze himself through that tiny little hole, and then I'd think about joining him.

With a shrug, Jack perched on the edge of the hole, legs dangling into the space beyond. Then he carefully lowered himself in. His legs, hips, and torso fit surprisingly well. It was his shoulders that were the problem. He didn't bat an eyelash. He simply maneuvered one arm through the hole with a weird ducking, twisting move, and the rest of him dropped through easily.

"All right, Morgan," he called up. "Move your ass. Moonlight's burning."

"Okay, okay." I swung my own legs into the cavity, my fingers gripping the sides of the manhole. "Moonlight's burning, my backside." I lowered myself slightly, then I let go and slid into empty space.

Chapter 32

Surprisingly, my hips fit through the manhole with only a minor amount of scraping. I'd have a lovely bruise come morning, though. The drop wasn't far, either, with Jack to catch me. He was very business-like and impersonal about touching me, which just made things more awkward than they had to be.

We were standing in a man-made tunnel. The ceiling was high enough we could both stand up easily in the space below the open manhole.

"Where are we?" I asked, gazing about as we moved deeper into the tunnel. Not that I could see a damn thing. It was pitch black away from the open manhole, and my eyes were taking their own sweet time adjusting. I wondered if using my powers too much weakened my natural abilities, or if I was just tired and needed a nap.

"The sewer system."

"Ew. Are you kidding me?" I reflexively yanked up a foot as though I could save my boots from the nastiness lurking in Paris's sewers. "Why didn't you tell me?"

"And what would you have done if I had?" From his tone, it was clear Jack didn't actually care about my answer.

"Steal somebody's rubber boots."

Jack barked a short laugh. "This is an unused part of the system. Don't worry. Anything down here has long since turned to dust."

"Wonderful," I muttered. I was standing in ancient poo. Could this day get any better?

"This way."

I wished I'd had a flashlight or something, but the only one I'd brought to France with me was a UV light. I didn't want to waste the batteries in case we ran into any vampires down in the bowels of the earth. My eyes adjusted fairly quickly as I followed Jack into the maze of tunnels that ran under the streets of Paris. We were in one of the older sections, eighteen-hundreds, maybe. The walls were made of uniformly cut stones, which arched smoothly overhead, all neatly mortared in place with as much care as if the mason had been building a palace. Somewhere nearby I could hear the trickle of water, and I caught a faint whiff of what was very much an active sewer system.

A short way up ahead, the tunnel was barred by an iron gate. The lock looked like a relic of the French Revolution or something, all big and blocky and covered in orange rust. Jack broke it easily, snapping the brittle old iron. As he pushed the gate open, the hinges creaked ominously. It was obvious no one had been this way in a very long time.

Beyond the gate lay a more modern tunnel with shiny metal pipework and caged fluorescent lights which were currently off. It was damper in this section, too; some of the walls seeping moisture. I wrinkled my nose at the stench.

"Are we there yet?"

"Almost." There was a hint of amusement in his voice.

After a few yards, the modern tunnel branched off in two directions. Jack took the right fork, me hot on his tail. The tunnel split a couple more times as it spread out beneath the city. Finally, Jack stopped at what I first mistook for a solid wall. On closer inspection, I realized there was a door in the wall. A very old door. Solid steel painted gray to blend in with the surrounding tiles. It was completely smooth without even a handle. It looked like it had been welded in place, but under the welds, I saw bumps that had once been hinges. At some point, this door had been operable.

"Now what?" I asked. The door probably weighed a ton. "Even you, oh mighty warrior, can't open this."

"No." A smile curved his lips. "But you can."

I gave him a look that spoke volumes about my assessment of his mental state. "Don't be an idiot. If you can't open that door, I sure as hell can't." Even channeling Darkness, the weight of that door would squash me flat. If I could even break it open in the first place.

His smile widened. "Morgan, have you ever seen a welder in action?"

"Only on TV. Why?" I was pretty sure watching *Flashdance* didn't count.

"How do they weld something in place?"

"With a...." I stopped, mouth hanging open. Holy shit. I was an idiot. I'd totally forgotten I was a freaking human blowtorch. "You're serious? You want me to try this?"

He nodded. "Unless you can think of a better way."

I couldn't. "How did you get through it last time you were here?"

He shook his head. "That was over two-hundred years ago, Morgan. This part of the tunnel was almost brand new and in full use. I didn't need to break in."

"If I do get it open, how are we going to hold it? It must weigh a ton."

"We don't need to hold it. We just need to get out of its way."

Still I hesitated.

"You can do this. You know you can."

I wasn't so sure about that, but what the heck. I stepped closer to the door. My fingers brushed over the old metal, searching out the welded bits. Make those suckers hot enough, and they'd fall to the floor, leaving the door free to move again. As long as Jack caught it, or pulled me out before it fell on my head, this should work.

I sucked in a deep breath of sewer-scented air. "Here goes nothing."

Pressing my fingers against the bumpy spots of welded metal, I closed my eyes and reached inside myself. All my powers looked up eagerly, excited to get out, but I was only playing with Fire today. I beckoned to it to join me. It needed no further coaxing.

In a hot surge, it leapt up and out, blasting through the palm of my hand in a huge fireball. Before it could let loose, I tugged it back, squeezing it down into focus. I didn't need a huge flame, I needed precision. A needle, not a crowbar.

I lay the fingers of both hands along the weld line on one side of the door, letting the Fire through in narrow pinpoints, but as hot as it wanted. The metal under my fingertips grew hotter and hotter until I thought it might burn them right off. I pulled my hands slightly away from the metal so my skin didn't burn. Even with a small gap between me and the door, the Fire jumped eagerly from my hands, greedily eating away at the weld.

Before long, the metal began to glow. It turned cherry red and then globs of welding material began to drip from the door. Chunks of glowing metal plopped to the floor, hissing against the moisture there.

"Good," Jack said. "Now here." He pointed to an area on the top edge of the door.

The door was low enough for me to reach if I stretched a little. Once more placing my fingertips against the weld, I willed the Fire to burn. Hotter, stronger, faster. The top weld went in half the time as the Fire inside me eagerly licked and ate at the door, hungry for more.

"Now here."

Once again I placed my fingers where he told me, wiling the Fire to do its work. My vision turned a sort of orangey yellow, as if I were looking through tinted glasses. Sweat beaded my forehead and upper lip, trickled down my back, and pooled at the base of my spine. I wasn't sure if it was from the heat, or the intensity of focus I was trying desperately to maintain. Maybe both. My muscles were shaking with fatigue, and my head was beginning to throb. My mouth felt like someone had stuffed hot cotton in it. Or week-old dirty socks.

This time, the Fire spilled over, heating not just the weld, but the metal around it. I was losing concentration, my grip on the Fire weakening. I had to hurry, or I wouldn't be able to pull it back in. Without the Marid around to stop the Fire, I'd burn out of control.

An image flashed into my mind: the dream I'd once had of another woman Kissed by Fire. The Fire had burned inside her so hotly, she'd nearly destroyed a city. Instead, she'd thrown herself off a cliff to be eaten by a dragon. Not exactly the way I wanted to go out. Besides, there weren't any dragons handy.

Forcing those images out of my head, I concentrated on the task at hand. Faster. I needed to go faster.

I gave up on focus and let the fire blast. Within seconds, a huge chunk of door had gone from cherry red to melting puddle. Good enough.

I leashed the Fire, willing it back inside me. It snarled and lashed out, wanting to keep playing, burning. It was hungry. I was hungry.

Yes, it hissed, *let me free.*

"No. Fucking. Way." Each word was squeezed out through gritted teeth past the utter exhaustion that nearly overwhelmed me. I sank to my knees, no longer able to stand, physically exhausted. I sensed my mind wasn't far behind.

With one last effort, I grabbed the Fire around its metaphorical throat and with what little energy I had left yanked it back inside me with the sheer brute force of my mind. I thrust it down into the place where the other powers lived and slammed the lid down tight.

The Fire safe inside me, I finally let go. Sliding completely to the floor, I curled into a fetal position. I was bathed in sweat, every muscle aching to the point of near numbness. I closed my eyes and let the blackness take me down.

Chapter 33

The world came back slowly. It was the scent that hit me first: musty and damp like everything else, but with a thread of something unusual underneath, something that didn't belong. It was spicy and exotic, fresh and green. I'd smelled it before, that odd mix of odors, but I couldn't quite put my finger on it. My mind was a swirly mass of confusion.

Next came the sounds: the drip of water, the scuff of a boot against hard ground, someone muttering rude words in French. Jack. That was right. I was down in the tunnels with Jack, who had used me as a human blowtorch.

I cracked an eyelid open, waiting for the painful rush of light. Except it didn't come. It was pitch black. Almost. I frowned as I realized the darkness around me was tinged with green. As my eyes slowly adjusted, the green grew more intense. I checked myself to make sure I wasn't channeling Earth power again. I wasn't. The faint green light wasn't coming from me, but from somewhere farther down the tunnel.

"You're awake."

I shifted my head so I could see Jack, wincing as he clicked on his flashlight. "Ouch. Could you turn that thing off?"

"Sorry."

The light switched off, plunging me back into the cool, green darkness. I let out a sigh of relief.

"How are you feeling?" His voice was a low rumble near my ear.

I repressed a shiver of awareness. I may have chosen Inigo, but apparently my body hadn't entirely caught up to my mind's decision yet. I flexed my fingers and toes, checking for any twinges of pain. "My head hurts like hell, but otherwise I think I'm okay. Please don't tell me I passed out."

"Okay, I won't."

Crap. I managed to heave myself into a sitting position. I felt weak and the muscles in my arms trembled as if holding up my own weight was too much for them. "Guess that little magic trick really took it out of me."

"It's getting stronger, you know," Jack said. "Your ability to channel the magic. Each time you use it, there's more." I could almost feel him frowning in the green darkness.

"Yeah," I admitted. "I know. But there's not a hell of a lot I can do about that, is there? Thanks to the amulet, I'm now a reservoir for every single lost Atlantean superpower." I didn't add that, for every step forward in controlling those superpowers, I seemed to take two steps back. One day I'd take a step back and there'd be no more going forward.

Jack didn't say anything. There was nothing to say. He was the one who'd brought us together in the first place: the amulet and me.

Okay, that wasn't fair. It had been Darroch who'd brought the Heart of Atlantis close enough for it to sense me, but Jack would have done it if he'd had the thing in his possession. It was his life's mission to find and protect the Key. He was, after all, the Guardian.

I managed to haul myself to my feet, using the wall to keep me upright. "Where's that green light coming from?"

"Somewhere up ahead."

I frowned, holding back a sarcastic reply. Sometimes I wanted to smack that man upside the head. "Is it normal down here to have green lights?"

"Not exactly. It's usually completely dark in this part of the underground. It's not open to tourists, and it's no longer used by the sewer workers. It was sealed off years ago, so there's no need for lights."

"Interesting. I'm thinking we should check it out."

Jack grunted what sounded like agreement as we moved down the tunnel toward the glow. I was glad for the darkness, as it meant I could lean a little more heavily against the stone wall without Jack noticing and going all caveman on me.

As we rounded a corner, the glow intensified, bathing everything in rich, emerald green. The spicy, fresh scent grew stronger, too. Honeysuckle, vanilla, and cinnamon twined around the more exotic scents of hibiscus and coffee. Beneath all that was something stranger and wilder. I couldn't quite put my finger on it, but I was pretty sure it was nothing of this world.

The answer was obvious. "The Other World."

"What?"

"Do you smell it?" I asked.

Jack sniffed. "Some flowery thing. Are you wearing perfume?"

"Right. I just pulled out a vial while I was unconscious and started spritzing myself in the middle of the sewer." If sarcasm could kill. "That's the scent of the Other World. The land of the Sidhe."

"Down here?" Jack ignored my testiness. "How is that even possible?"

I didn't answer. I knew about as much as he did.

Moving through an archway, I stopped, Jack nearly barreling into me from behind. I held up a hand to forestall any grumbling, my eyes fixed on the vision ahead of me.

The archway opened into a small brick-walled room. Opposite was another archway leading on into the dark, but in the middle of the room, blocking the pathway, a disc hovered, suspended in midair. It swirled and shimmered, the free-floating green circle reminding me of a wormhole from one of those science fiction movies.

I stepped a little closer, feeling the tug of its energy pulling me. The scent was strongest here, emanating from the glowing disc. I could have sworn I heard the delicate sound of flutes from the other side of the disc.

"It's a portal to the Other World." I couldn't keep the awe from my voice. The previous times I'd traveled to fairy land, it had been because the queen pulled me there. I hadn't needed a portal, but I recognized it from my dream.

"A portal under the streets of Paris?" Jack sounded dubious.

"Why not?" I held out my hand, palm toward the swirling disc. The energy from the portal gave it a gentle tug. This was it. Finally. A way in. I could face the Queen at last. Demand answers.

"Careful, Morgan," Jack warned. "We don't know why that thing is here."

I smiled. "Oh, yes, we do. The portal is here because Alister and Darroch are hiding out with the Fairy Queen."

He seemed startled. "Why?"

"No idea. But I'm going to find out."

Between one breath and the next, I stepped through the portal.

***

It was as though every bone in my body was being ripped out through my skin and smashed to dust. The air was sucked from my lungs, the water sapped from my eyes. I couldn't see, couldn't breathe. Even my heart stopped, the awful pressure squeezing it until every drop of blood had leaked out, leaving an empty husk.

Then I crashed to the ground in a heap, and everything came rushing back. I sucked in a lungful of flowery scented air, coughing and choking on nothing. I pressed a fist against my chest over my heart, which was hammering so hard, I thought it might explode. I curled the fingers of my other hand into the ground, sinking them into soft soil and tender green things. Real. This was real.

I managed to roll out of the way a split second before Jack crashed to the ground exactly where I had been kneeling. I lay there in the lush green grass staring at him, willing my body to move. It ignored me.

I was able to flop over on my back, staring at the sky as Jack coughed and gasped beside me. I frowned. How odd. Unlike the sky back home, the sky of the Other World was more green than blue. Everything around me, as far as I could see, was a rich, lush green. No bright flowers or birds, just leaves and vines and bushy things. The last time I'd been to the Other World, it had looked nothing like this. It had been all black, cold marble with a vein of gold running through it. This place, on the other hand, was warm and alive.

I dragged in another deep lungful of exotic air. I could definitely smell flowers, so there must be some somewhere. Spices, too. Vanilla and coffee. Chocolate maybe. Other things I couldn't identify. But it all smelled as though a bakery had exploded and taken a florist shop with it.

I rolled up to my knees. Somebody was definitely playing a flute. The tune was jaunty and haunting at the same time. A dragonfly buzzed near my face, flashing like a ruby in the sunlight. I brushed it away only to realize it wasn't an insect at all, but a small, winged human-like creature. It grinned at me, flashing fangs that would have done a vampire proud. Then with a giggle, it zoomed off to disappear into the jungle of trees and vines.

I staggered to my feet, determined to avoid any more such creatures. The world spun for a second, and then righted itself. Good. I wasn't going to fall over. Or hurl.

I closed my eyes, willing strength back into my body. That's when I felt them: my powers. They were hovering just beneath the surface, ready to bust out and do their thing whenever I willed it.

"Impossible," I muttered under my breath as I opened my eyes. During both of my previous visits to the Other World, my powers hadn't worked. Not even a tiny bit. My hunter strength had been there, but the Atlantean powers had vanished. Now, if anything, they were stronger than ever.

"What the hell?" Jack sat up next to me, one hand on his forehead. He winced against the light.

"Exactly what I'd like to know." The strange voice came out of nowhere.

I spun around, rather unsteadily, and stared at the newcomer. He was tall, blond, and very nicely built, but his face was shifting through incarnations so fast, I was afraid that I might throw up after all. I had to stare at his right shoulder to avoid the dizzying morph of his features. Behind him ranged a dozen high-ranking and heavily armed Sidhe.

"Shit," I mumbled, glancing at his shiny armor and wicked looking sword.

"I prefer Kalen. Captain of the Queen's Guard. Please." He flashed a smile that left me feeling decidedly icky. "Come with me. The Queen desires an audience."

"And if I say no?"

A dozen swords cleared a dozen sheaths. "That," Kalen said in an icy voice, "would be unwise."

Chapter 34

Jack and I marched along the narrow path behind Kalen and his gang of merry men. Two more guards walked behind us, swords at the ready should we decide to get feisty. That was unlikely, seeing as how Kalen had bound our hands in front of us with some kind of fuzzy green vine. If I so much as thought about escaping, the vine tightened until my fingers turned purple. It was like it was psychic or something. Too bad we didn't have this stuff in our world. I sure could have used it.

If that wasn't enough, our weapons hadn't come through with us. It wasn't entirely a surprise. The other times I'd been to the land of the Sidhe, my weapons had stayed behind in my world, something about human metal being anathema to the fae. Apparently, human metal simply couldn't pass through the barrier between our worlds. No doubt our blades were still back in the sewer tunnel in Paris.

Escape was definitely out of the question. At least for now.

Giant trees loomed on either side of the footpath, trunks as thick as my car was long. Their long branches swept over us, creating a tunnel of greenery. It was as though we moved through green twilight. Here and there, hidden within the dense green leaves, I caught sight of dainty cream-colored blossoms. Yellow eyes stared at us from deeper within the forest, and brightly colored bird-like creatures flitted about, filling the air with their songs. I recognized the flute sounds I'd heard earlier.

The air was warm and a little muggy, almost jungle-like. Kalen and his men appeared unmoved by the heat despite their heavy armor, while my clothes stuck uncomfortably to my sweaty skin. I repressed a yawn. The heavy air was making me unusually sleepy. Or maybe it was the flowers. Who knew what kind of properties could be found in the flora of the Other World? I wondered if I could sneak some back for Eddie. He'd be delighted to study them.

More of the little dragonfly fairy creatures with fangs fluttered around our heads, dipping and dive-bombing us in flashes of bright reds, oranges, and pinks. Their shrieks of hilarity threatened to burst my eardrums. Oh, for a fly swatter. Or a really big bug zapper.

One of them landed on my shoulder and tried to sink his fangs into my skin. Without even turning, Kalen snapped out something in Sidhe. With a tiny squeal, the fairy creature took off like the hounds of hell were on his ass. Guess I owed Kalen one. No telling what that mini monster would have done to me. For all I knew, its fangs were filled with poison.

"This is insane," Jack muttered. "We're just going along with this?"

"We don't exactly have a choice. Kalen left the portal guarded, we have no weapons, and there's no getting out of these damn vines. Not to mention we have no idea what kind of creatures are lurking in that forest ready to eat us. So for now, we play along and look for an opening." I didn't mention I really wanted to see the Queen.

He snorted. "You know the minute we're in front of the Queen, we're dead."

"You are, maybe. But she has other plans for me."

"Gee, thanks," Jack said dryly. "That makes me feel all warm and fuzzy."

I flashed him a grin. "Don't worry, Jack. I'll protect you."

My feet and back were aching by the time we finally broke free of the forest and stepped out onto a wide, grassy plain. The path cut its way through the grass, sloping away until it ended at a ravine. On the other side, jagged black rocks rose from the ground to form a natural barrier, and rising from within the thickest part of the rock forest was a castle.

"Behold." Kalen gestured grandly. "The Palace of the Queen of the Sidhe."

It was straight out of a fairytale: soaring turrets, princess towers, flying buttresses. The palace was a study in the delicate and whimsical. Except every inch of it was black as coal and inside dwelled the creature who'd taken Inigo from me.

***

"Ah, Kalen, what have you brought me?"

I'd know Morgana's voice anywhere.

"Interlopers, my queen," Kalen said with a flourish and a bow.

The Sidhe guards shoved Jack and me to the floor. My knees hit the familiar black marble with a shock of pain that brought tears to my eyes. Bastards. I glared up at my guard, promising myself he'd be the first to pay. He sneered at me, his face morphing quickly into a new incarnation.

The Queen was lounging on a massive black throne that seemed to rise straight out of the marble floor, as if it were all one single, solid piece. Her left leg was draped over one arm of the throne. A dainty bare foot with toenails painted hot pink swung casually back and forth. Morgana's strawberry-blond hair fell in wildly disheveled curls all around her as though she'd just hauled her ass out of bed and hadn't bothered to comb it. She had on one of her trademark Grecian style dresses, though one of the straps was dipping so low, she was very much in danger of going truly Grecian and flashing boob. Knowing the queen, she probably couldn't care less. Or rather, she knew exactly how such exposure would affect everyone around her, and would wait for just the right moment to have a wardrobe malfunction.

Behind the throne a dozen different fae creatures stood, holding various items the queen clearly thought important. The creatures were definitely not Sidhe, but from lower castes of fairy. The one currently kneeling next to the throne was a striking female who looked more-or-less human, but had gold skin and hair to match. And by gold, I mean the stuff that comes out of the ground. Actual gold color, not the dark yellow people refer to as gold. She glittered and shone like she was made of the precious metal. Even the box she held was gold. The only thing not gold was her simple ankle-length robe, which was as black as the marble all around us.

My attention was snagged by a familiar figure trying to blend in with the exotic beings around him: Brent Darroch. With his smarmy good looks and perfectly tailored clothing, I'd recognize the bastard anywhere. He caught me looking and shot me a sardonic smile. Jackass. I didn't see Alister Jones.

I turned back to the queen. "Hello, Morgana." It was daring, calling her by one of her true names, but it was the one power I had over her. I needed every trick at my disposal if Jack and I were going to come out of this alive.

"Morgan. How lovely of you to visit again." She smiled, her plump pink lips parting to reveal the tiny gap between her front teeth. "It has been an age since you were last within my realm."

"I called. I guess you were busy."

The smile widened. "Oh, yes. A bit." Morgana reached into the gold box held up by the gold girl. When the Queen brought out her hand, she was holding a piece of dark chocolate. She popped it in her mouth, savoring it for a moment. "I do have a kingdom to run."

I snorted. "More like a war to start. What the hell were you thinking, getting into it with the djinn?"

Her face turned into a mask of ice as she went rigid with fury. "Choose your words carefully, human. My patience wears thin."

The ice took hold of my veins as she held my gaze. My stomach churned and my legs turned to jelly. I was drowning, wallowing in fear.

I shook my head. No. This was Morgana's doing. I could see it now, clear as day. She was making me feel afraid. Yes, she was more powerful than I. Yes, she could squash me like a bug. But I was not without power of my own, and if Morgana had wanted me dead, she'd have killed me long ago.

"Guess what?" I snapped. "So does mine. You used me, Morgana, and that is not something I forget. Or forgive."

"It is not up to you to choose forgiveness." Her voice was a hiss, reminding me of the viper she was. "I am queen here." Her tone indicated she considered herself queen pretty much anywhere.

"Are you? Really? If you're so damn powerful, then why hitch your star to the likes of Alister Jones and Brent Darroch? I know you and Alister tampered with Jade Vincent's memories. Father Nicolas's, too." I had no proof of the later, but there was no doubt in my mind she was in it up to her gap-toothed smile. "Are you so weak you need humans and vampires to do your dirty work, now, Your *Majesty*?" Holy shit. Had I crossed the line? I half expected her to smite me on the spot.

The queen was shaking with fury, her cheeks flushed, eyes ice cold. She clenched her dainty hands into fists. "How dare you. You have no right...."

"I have every right," I interrupted. If you're going to poke the beehive, might as well do it with gusto. "You killed the man I love." Morgana didn't need to know Inigo was still technically alive. "If that weren't enough, you used me to start a war. When you pick a fight with the djinn, you pick a fight with humanity. That makes this my business."

Morgana narrowed her eyes. A flush rode high on her cheeks. She trembled with barely repressed rage. Oh, yeah, she was pissed.

"Morgan." The warning tone in Jack's voice was clear. So was my intention to ignore him.

"Do you see him?" I kept my voice low, pitched only for Jack's ears. I could only hope the others didn't hear me.

"Darroch? Yes."

"Good, when I give the signal, grab him." I had no doubt that even bound, Jack could easily overcome Brent Darroch. "Then the two of you get the hell out of Dodge."

The entire time we were talking, I'd kept my eyes on the Queen as she struggled to overcome her anger. Slowly, she sat up straight, feet planted firmly on the floor. She leaned forward, hands on the arms of her throne. "Listen carefully, human," she spat. The expression on her face was so cold, so inhuman, it made me shiver. "You are only alive because I will it so. Cross me, and that will change. I have no compunction about killing you and everyone you have ever met. You are nothing but insects to me. Do we understand each other?"

"Perfectly." Outwardly I smiled, but inwardly I was calling my powers. Slowly. Softly. "But know this, Morgana, you will pay for what you did to Inigo. And if you harm one more person, human or djinn, friend or stranger, I will come after you. I will bring down your throne, your house, your fucking kingdom."

She laughed, but there was little humor in it. "You and whose army, human?"

"I don't need an army."

With that I let the Fire rip. It burned through my bonds so fast, they were nothing but ash in less than a second. Darkness surged, and I whirled, grabbing the sword of the Sidhe guard closest to me straight out of its sheath before he had a chance to react. A single thrust through the heart with the short blade, and he was dead on the floor, the spreading pool of crimson a splash of color against the endless black marble of the castle.

No one moved. The entire court, including the queen, sat with their mouths hanging open. So I did the first thing that came to mind. I threw a fireball straight at the throne.

The queen managed to deflect the fireball, but just barely. It hit the silk draperies hanging behind her, turning them into a raging bonfire.

Chaos erupted. Fae creatures ran, jumped, slithered, and flew here and there, tripping each other and the guards. The gold girl cowered beside the throne, her gold box fallen, spilling chocolates across the floor. The queen was shouting orders, but no one could hear amid the pandemonium.

The next fireball was smaller, but better aimed. It hit the queen full in the chest. Her clothes and hair went up in flames, and her skin crinkled black. She screamed, a sound filled with rage and pain.

I felt a tiny thrill of triumph before a second guard lunged at me. A single stroke with my newly acquired fairy blade, and his head separated from his body, spattering me with warm blood. Gods, I loved wielding a Sidhe sword. It was so light and insanely sharp. On the off chance I survived this, I was definitely bringing it back with me. It could replace the blades that were still lying in the Paris catacombs.

I glanced up in time to see Kalen ushering a completely healed Morgana from the throne room. Her moon-pale skin was unmarred, and her strawberry blonde locks were already growing back. She was also buck naked. She didn't appear to be happy about leaving, but she went. The pair slipped through a doorway partially hidden behind the burning draperies. The door sealed behind them, leaving a seamless wall. Figures the bitch would sacrifice her people to save her own skin.

Not that I could kill her. She was immortal. But I could sure as hell make her hurt.

The pounding of feet alerted me to the arrival of more of the queen's guard. At least a dozen heavily armed Sidhe flooded the throne room from the main entrance. A dozen more spilled through side doors. Shit. This was not good.

"Morgan! This way."

Jack waved at me from a corner of the room. He had used his badass Templar skills to get free of his bonds and grab Darroch around the neck. I didn't see any exits over there, but "stand together or die alone," and all that. I ran for the corner, hacking wildly at anything that crossed my path.

"There's no way out." My breath was coming fast and hard. My arms were tiring from the effort of wielding the fairy sword, despite its light weight.

"Here," Jack interrupted, pointing to the floor.

I frowned. "Where?"

"Hold him." Jack thrust Darroch my way.

I grabbed the man, pressing the edge of my blade rather closer to his nether regions than strictly necessary. "Hey, Brent, nice to see you again."

Darroch blanched, but otherwise remained as unruffled as ever. "Morgan. Likewise."

"Uh-huh."

Jack seemed to find what he was looking for. Suddenly, a section of the floor popped up, revealing a flight of stairs leading below. "Escape hatch."

"Excellent. Assholes first," I said, shoving Darroch down through the hatch, keeping the point of the blade pressed to his back. Jack followed close behind, closing the hatch and plunging us into darkness.

Chapter 35

We'd maybe gone eight or ten feet down the tunnel when Darroch suddenly let out a very unmanly squeak. Next thing I knew, the ground beneath me disappeared, and I was plummeting through empty space. I let out a shriek so loud, I nearly deafened myself.

Except I wasn't quite plummeting. It was more like zipping along incredibly fast, like on those water slides at amusement parks. There was definitely a slick surface under my butt. There must have been a slide or chute under the castle. It twisted and turned and occasionally dropped a couple feet, making for one hell of a ride through the blackness.

With Darroch screeching in front and Jack hollering behind, I gritted my teeth and kept the sharp blade of the fairy sword well away from me, determined to survive the ride. I would not completely freak out. Flying along in the pitch black to gods knew where was not my idea of a good time. Not to mention, once we came out the other side, we would be nearly weaponless, totally lost, and at the mercy of the Other World.

Abruptly, we exploded from complete darkness into bright daylight. Then we really were flying...falling. I let out an embarrassingly girly shriek seconds before I plunged into ice cold water.

I kept my fingers firmly wrapped around the sword hilt as the water closed over my head. Down I went through the murky water until my feet hit the muddy bottom. I pushed off, sending myself back toward the surface. Numbed limbs flailing, I struggled toward the edge of the water. I hauled myself out of the pool and onto the soft grass in time to see Darroch disappear into the woods. "Shit. Dammit. Jack, I'm going after him."

I didn't bother waiting for Jack's reply as I staggered off after Darroch. No way was I letting that bastard get away.

My wet clothes hugged my skin and chilled my bones, making it difficult to move quickly, but if I was having problems, so was my quarry. I plunged into the cool green dimness of the forest. All around me, butterflies fluttered and flitted. I didn't look too closely at them. The dragonfly creatures had been bad enough.

The trees and other flora grew thick and lush, making it hard to find any sort of path. A vine reached out as if to wrap itself around me. I dodged, slashing at it with my sword. The half I severed from the plant withered instantly. The rest of it crept back into the undergrowth as though afraid. I continued on my journey, heading in the direction I'd seen Darroch go. The sneaky bastard was fast.

Ahead of me, I could just make out a flash of his pale hair. I charged through a narrow gap between shrubberies, long branches swiping bloody trails across my bare neck and face. Thank goodness for leather jackets or my arms would have been sliced to ribbons. I hissed out a few choice swear words. I was moving too fast to use the sword as a machete. What I wouldn't give to be able to part the forest like Moses parting the proverbial Red Sea.

As if it had heard my thoughts, the trees and bushes began to bend away. They parted, letting me by unmolested, leaving a clear path to Brent Darroch's retreating back.

"What the hell?" I wasn't even channeling Earth, yet the Other World flora was definitely acting as if I were. I hesitated for a moment before deciding to just go with it. I'd figure out why later, provided the spooky-ass forest didn't eat me first.

The sound of Jack crashing and cussing his way through the underbrush made me grin. He was catching up.

I took off again down the path made by the retreating plant life, narrowing the gap between me and Darroch. With one last surge of speed, I dropped the sword and leaped the final distance, landing on his back and taking him to the ground with an audible *oof.* We went tumbling through the bushes, rolling to a stop in the midst of a small glade.

"Stay down, you asshat. Or so help me, I'll break every bone in your body."

"Fine. I'm down." Darroch spat out a few blades of grass. He lay there panting for a minute with me still sitting on top him. "Will you please let me sit up so I can breathe?"

"Don't try anything funny." I clambered off him.

"Or what?" He sneered, his Julian Sands good looks turning ugly as he brushed random bits of greenery off his clothing with an elegant hand. I noticed his nails were professionally manicured. "You're unarmed."

I smiled. "You think I need weapons?" Not to mention there was a fairy sword laying a few steps away.

That made him go a little pale and sweaty. I turned my attention from Darroch to our surroundings. We'd somehow made it back to the place where Jack and I had come through the portal to the Other World.

I frowned. Something wasn't right. "Where's the portal?"

Darroch glanced around, an expression of panic crossing his usually haughty face. "It's not here."

"Yes," I said dryly. "I can see that. What I want to know is, where is it?"

"I have no idea." He seemed to be on the verge of a complete meltdown. Clearly he hadn't expected this turn of events any more than I had. "It's supposed to be here. It's always been here. She must have moved it."

"She?" I had a bad feeling.

"The queen, of course. Only she can control the portal. You have to find it. You have to make her tell you what she did with it." Yep. Definitely panicked.

"Listen buddy," I said, keeping my voice calm and low like I was talking to an unstable person, which maybe I was. "I don't have to do anything. Why are you so worked up, anyway? You're the one in cahoots with Her Majesty."

His expression turned dark. "Maybe. But that doesn't mean I want to be stuck here. If you think this place is all fun and games, you're as much a fruitcake as she is."

Jack suddenly crashed out of the bushes, interrupting my train of thought. He saw my fairy sword on the ground and snatched it up in one hand. "Where's the portal?" He glanced from me to Darroch and back again, as if one of us might be hiding the damn thing in our back pockets.

"Apparently, the queen moved it while we were off having our little huddle. He," I pointed to Darroch, "says only the Queen can control the portal."

"Crap." Jack ran a hand through his hair before handing me my sword. I nodded my thanks. Every inch of him was vibrating with frustration. "So only she knows where it is."

"Not exactly," Darroch interrupted. We both whirled on him.

"Explain," Jack barked.

For a moment, I thought Darroch wouldn't tell us. He must have decided we were the lesser of two evils, or maybe we were the best way for him to get what he wanted. In any case, he finally nodded.

"The queen is the only one who can control the portals, but anyone in the fairy realm knows where the portal is. It's as though they can sense its location."

"We're in the fairy realm," Jack pointed out. "I don't know about you, but I sure can't sense any portal."

"You also have to be *of* the fairy realm," Darroch explained impatiently.

"So all we need to do is find one of the fae creatures and make them tell us where the portal is," I said.

Darroch nodded. "Yes. Exactly."

I imagined it was easier said than done. Except...

"Those damn dragonfly creatures," I said. "They kept wanting to bite me. Maybe if I caught one of them?"

"And how exactly are you going to do that?" Jack asked. "We have no weapons except your sword. Nothing to capture them with."

"Oh, ye of little faith." I grinned. "I'm going to try something. Guard him." I nodded to Darroch before stepping away from the men, closer to the woods.

An interesting thought had wormed its way into my brain. I had wished for the forest to open up and let me pass, and it had. The first two trips to fairy land, my powers hadn't worked, and now they did. I carried Earth power within me, and the Sidhe were made of Earth power. Heck, the whole Other World ran on Earth power. It was the very essence of Earth magic made manifest. Perhaps I could draw those little fanged fairies to me.

I took a deep breath and let a hint of my Earth power out of me. My skin began to shimmer as green tendrils of magic worked their way across my body. I focused my thoughts on the winged fairy creatures, imagining their colorful wings and tiny little fangs, and waited.

At first there was nothing. Then, one by one, I saw little splashes of bright color flitting closer and closer. With a smile I held out my hand. Dozen of the tiny creatures hovered above my palm, mesmerized by the shimmering green aura surrounding me. Their tiny voices chittered with both excitement and fear.

One of the females grew brave enough to move a bit closer. The daring creature alighted on my hand, feet so delicate it felt like the tickle of butterfly wings. Faster than a blink, I closed my fingers around her. The rest of the dragonfly creatures scattered as the one in my hand started shrieking. I half expected her to bite me, but oddly, she didn't. Instead she wriggled around, letting out that ear-piercing scream over and over.

"Shut up."

She went silent, staring up at me from between the gaps in my fingers, her enormous eyes like one of those Asian tarsier primates, only this creature's eyes were a bright emerald green and took up half her face. She hissed at me, flashing her miniature pointy teeth.

"Put those fangs away."

Cowed, she did what I told her. She let out a mewling sound, cowering inside the cage of my hand.

"I want you to do one simple task for me. Then I'll let you go unharmed to rejoin your friends."

She stared at me blankly. I wasn't fooled. It was a defense mechanism, and given half the chance, she'd bite my hand off. Still, I had no doubt there was one thing she couldn't resist, no matter how much she might want to. I infused my next words with the full weight of my Earth power, my voice echoing with it.

"Show me the portal."

Chapter 36

Thanks to the little fairy creature, we found the portal deeper in the woods of the Other World. It dropped us on the steps of the Sacre Couer. Not exactly what I expected, but at least it was still the middle of the night, so no one noticed three people magically appearing out of nowhere. Granted, most Parisians wouldn't have batted an eyelash, but one didn't want to upset the tourists.

"If we head down to one of the main streets, we should be able to find a taxi," Jack suggested.

"And pay the driver, how?" I asked. "We left our money back at the hotel." Along with our phones and IDs. We hadn't planned to go joyriding when we'd set out for the catacombs.

"One of us stays with the car while the other runs up and gets the money." Jack's tone was that of a person speaking to someone very, very dense.

I felt like smacking myself in the forehead. I hadn't even thought of it, mostly because my lack of French would have led to one pissed off driver. Jack, however, could easily explain.

"Okay, fine." I grabbed Darroch by the arm. His hands were still tied together with vines from the Other World. They seemed to operate just fine in ours. "And while we walk, Brent, you can tell us what the heck you and your buddy are up to with the Fairy Queen."

"I wouldn't call him my buddy." Darroch stumbled a little as I jerked him along beside me down the steps, yet somehow he managed to maintain his usual air of haughty disdain.

"Then what would you call him?" Jack demanded, following us closely.

Darroch heaved a sigh. "We were friends once. But Alister Jones is too busy plotting world domination and mass murder to consider things like friendship."

"Oh, you mean like you?" I snapped.

"It seemed a good idea at the time." It was clear from Darroch's tone he still thought it was a good idea. One he'd be happy to reinstate given half the chance. "In any case, Jones used me and the Queen of the Sidhe to get what he wanted, then left us behind to..."

"Wait a minute." I stopped dead in the middle of the street. "Alister double-crossed you? And Morgana?"

Darroch flinched a little at the use of the Fairy Queen's true name. "Yes."

"How is he not stone cold dead?" I should know. Not that I'd actually betrayed her, mind you. More like the other way around, but Morgana had an odd way of looking at things. "The queen does not take betrayal lightly."

Darroch sighed, stumbling to a halt beside me on the sidewalk. "Under normal circumstances he would be dead, but she can't kill Alister until we find out what he did with the book."

"Whoa. Wait a minute. What the hell are you talking about?" Jack grabbed him by the arm. Hard, too, if Darroch's expression was anything to go by.

"Listen." Darroch glanced around as if he thought someone might be spying on us. "Get me somewhere safer than the middle of the street, and I'll clue you in. Deal?"

Jack and I glanced at each other. "Okay," I said. "Deal. Just tell me one thing."

Darroch raised an eyebrow, waiting.

"Why are you willing to tell us anything? You haven't exactly been cooperative in the past." Understatement of the year.

Darroch's expression turned grim. "Believe me, what Alister has planned is far, far worse than anything you could possibly imagine. He needs to be stopped. And I imagine you're one of the few who might actually be able to do it."

That was ominous. I tried to get Darroch to explain further, but he refused until we were somewhere he considered safe. He kept silent through the cab ride back to the hotel and up the elevator to my room. When we were inside, the door locked and bolted behind us, I shoved him down on the bed.

"Okay. Spill," I said, standing in front of him with my arms crossed, trying to give him my best Kabita 'look.' "What were you and the queen up to? And how does Alister figure into it?"

"Many years ago, the queen and I met under unusual circumstances."

I started to interrupt to ask what circumstances, but Darroch shook his head.

"It doesn't matter. What does matter was we found we had similar agendas."

"Which were?" Though I could pretty much guess.

"Power, of course. For me, it was to attain the abilities I'd been denied, thanks to my *human* blood." The way he said "human" made it sound dirty and disgusting.

His explanation made sense, though. Despite Darroch's Atlantean DNA, he didn't have the smallest speck of power. And he wanted it. Bad. It was the reason he'd stolen the Heart of Atlantis from Jack in the first place, and later kidnapped me. He'd wanted the power of the amulet for himself.

"And the queen?" Jack asked.

Darroch shrugged. "The queen claims she wants to bring her people back to what she feels is their rightful place in this world."

I stared at him in horror. The Sidhe had existed in a time before humans had evolved. In fact, one of the reasons they'd withdrawn to the Other World was that both species had developed to a point where they could no longer occupy the same space without destroying each other. And now there were more species than just humans to worry about. "You have got to be kidding me."

"I am not."

"But the djinn, dragons, humans... This planet can no longer sustain the Sidhe. She would destroy us all." I felt like I was on the verge of panic. The thought was truly monstrous.

Darroch carefully draped one leg over the other, smoothing out the creases in his trouser legs. "Believe me, the thought crossed my mind, but we came to an understanding. One we could both live with."

"Which was?" Jack prodded.

"It's not important." Darroch flicked an imaginary piece of lint from his knee. "What is important is we began to put the pieces in place, preparing for the day when we could make our vision of a new Earth a reality."

"Jade." It hit me all of a sudden. "It wasn't Alister I saw in my dream with the queen. It was you. The two of you altered Jade's memories."

"Yes," Darroch admitted. "That was one of our initial steps in the process. For the next, we needed Alister."

"Why?"

"He has technology and information which are useful to us."

"The soul vamp technology." It was a guess, but I was sure I was on the right track.

Darroch gave me a creepy smile. "Yes, but that wasn't all. Alister forced us to work with him after he used Jade to his advantage. She was a lost, angry child, and he made her believe he had her best interests at heart." Darroch let out an elegant snort.

"What exactly did Alister want from you?" I asked. I could understand why they might need something from him, but Alister was not the type to share glory.

"My method for controlling the vampires."

The entire room spun for a minute. I braced myself against the cheap dresser. "But he knows how to control vamps. He's the one who stole the technology from the SRA."

Darroch's smile grew even creepier, if that were possible. "Alister knows how to shove a soul into the body of a vampire with stolen technology and brute force. He does not know how to control them. We...needed each other." Darroch carefully smoothed back his white-blond hair. "Unfortunately, once Alister had what he wanted, he disappeared, along with the technology *and* the book." He nodded in Jack's direction. "Now I am back to square one."

"What does Alister want with the book?" My brain felt like it was spinning in seven different directions.

"To use it, of course." Darroch's tone told me he thought I was a moron. No surprise there. Darroch had always thought he was the brightest crayon in the box, never mind that I'd kicked his ass. Twice.

"What's in the book? Why do you guys want it?"

Darroch frowned. "We don't know specifically. What we do know is it's a key."

The key to the key.

I leaned in, staring him straight in the eye. I needed to know. "What does it have to do with me?"

This time his smile was genuine. "Everything."

I swallowed, half afraid to ask. Jack had no such fear. "What do you mean?"

Darroch's expression was enigmatic. "Let's just say, without the little hunter here, all would be lost. So, the Queen and I created a backup plan."

Feeling a little wobbly, I sank into the armchair next to the bed. Man, I needed a drink. "Jade."

"Again, yes. She was supposed to be our backup plan. Just in case."

"Then why the hit?" I asked, rubbing a hand over my face, suddenly exhausted. Nothing made sense to me.

"I don't understand." Darroch appeared genuinely confused.

"Someone put a hit out on Morgan," Jack explained. "Was it you?"

"Ah." Darroch's expression cleared. "No. Definitely not. We would prefer to use the original Key. The backup was simply that, a backup. An insurance plan. My guess is, the hit is Alister's doing. He has very specific goals, and Jade is far more biddable than Morgan." He said it like it was a compliment. I guess, in a weird way, it was.

"But why hire someone to kill her?" Jack asked.

"The only way for Jade to become the Key is for Morgan to die."

Freaking brilliant. "You still haven't told us what Alister's plan is. Why it's so much worse than yours or the queen's."

"Like I said, I simply want my birthright."

"Believe me," I said with a sigh. "It's not all it's cracked up to be."

Darroch gave me a long once-over. "Be that as it may, this is what I want. The queen wants to bring her people back to reclaim their land. She's convinced it's possible. It may be a bit...sticky for a while, but things have a way of working themselves out. She's been banished from this world for a long time. You know what it's like to miss home."

That I did. But just because you wanted to go home, didn't mean you could. "Go on."

"Alister." Darroch shook his head. "Alister wants more. So much more. He wants to rule the world, and he's willing to kill billions to do it. He wants to unleash a plague of vampirism on the planet. With his technology and what I taught him, he could control them all. And with the book he can, theoretically, unlock the Key. He would be unstoppable."

"Holy God," Jack breathed.

Darroch continued, "Alister has two problems. First of all, he doesn't yet know how to read the book, and therefore has no idea how to unlock the Key."

"And second?" I had a bad feeling.

Darroch gave me a pointed look. "You're still alive."

"Wonderful."

"I did try, you know. To protect you." He said it with some pride, as if he'd done something special and worthy of note.

"Excuse me?" Was he serious?

"The soul vampire you killed in Notre Dame? He was the last of mine. I sent him to watch you. I knew it was only a matter of time until Alister sent someone else, and I was trying to prevent your death."

I snorted. "Why? If you have Jade, what's the point?"

"In truth, Jade is Alister's creature. There is only so much we can do with her. The queen was hoping to bring you around to her way of thinking."

"Lord, she must be batshit crazy if she thinks she can do that. Inigo..."

Darroch held up his hand. "I know what she did. I told her she made a critical error in judgment, but the queen is not human. She does not understand love."

As if he did. "So it was Alister who got you out of Area 51?"

Darroch nodded. "With a little help from the queen."

"The portal. She opened it inside your prison bubble."

Darroch didn't answer, but I knew I was right. I turned to Jack. "What should we do with him?" I jabbed a finger at Darroch. "He can't go back to Area 51. She'd just get him out again." Or kill him, which might not be a bad thing, but it wouldn't be a right thing.

"You could let me go," Darroch suggested. "I'm on your side. Well, more on your side than Alister is."

"Not a snowball's chance in hell, Darroch."

He shrugged. "Worth a shot."

Jack pulled out his cellphone. "I'll call JP. He knows people who can help with difficult situations." He kept his voice low so Darroch couldn't hear him. "This time we'll put him somewhere no one will find him."

Chapter 37

We pawned Darroch off on JP's mysterious friends, and they'd hustled him into a black van and disappeared down the cobblestone street. The sun was just peeking over the horizon. I guessed France had its own version of Area 51. Leaving Jack to his own devices, I locked myself in my hotel room. I needed a long hot shower, food, and sleep. In that order. Instead, I found a visitor.

"Hello, Morgan." She sat primly in the armchair next to the window so the rising sun could spill artfully over her, setting her strawberry blonde hair afire.

"Hello, Your Majesty. I don't remember inviting you here." For the first time since I'd met the Queen of the Sidhe, I didn't feel a single ounce of fear. I was either getting braver, or I was an idiot. I was betting on the latter.

"I think it's time we talk." Morgana carefully arranged her nearly see-through gown so it draped perfectly over her slim, pale legs.

"Yes, I agree," I said, propping my hands on my hips and keeping my fingers close to the blades hidden in my waistband. Not that they'd help against the Fairy Queen, but they made me feel better. "I think you need to explain to me what the hell you're up to."

The queen's features hardened into icy stillness for a split second before she beamed at me. "Why, nothing at all."

"Don't lie, Morgana," I bit out.

She turned white with fury. "You dare much, hunter," she snarled.

I moved closer, so close she could probably feel my breath on her face. "That's because I've finally realized something."

Morgana raised one reddish-gold eyebrow. "And what is that?"

"That Alister ditched you as surely as he ditched Darroch. Darroch thinks the two of you were partners, but I'm betting you were playing both sides to get what you wanted. Not that it matters now. Whatever the three of you were planning, it's over. And now," I placed my hands on the arms of her chair so she was bracketed in, my face mere inches from hers, "you need me. Whatever you were doing to try and circumvent my cooperation didn't work, and now you have to work with me whether you like it or not."

Her expression was back to imperious ice queen, but she no longer frightened me. Because I had realized something she hadn't, something I should have realized during my sojourn in the Other World.

"How dare you," Morgana hissed. "I could rip you asunder. Destroy the very molecules of your being."

"You could try," I said with a smile. "But don't forget, you need me. And if you do forget that, you should remember this one other little thing."

"And what is that?" She made a pretense of disinterest, but I knew she was glued to my every word.

"I control the fae."

She blinked. "Excuse me?"

"Earth magic, Morgana. It flows in my veins." I held my hand out and let my Earth power trickle out. It shimmered along my skin like a green mist sprinkled with fairy dust. The queen turned even paler, if that were possible.

"It cannot be," she whispered.

"Apparently, it is." I pulled the magic back, letting it sink into my skin. Fortunately, it had decided to play nice today. "You see, I learned something today, oh Queen of the Sidhe."

"What would that be?" Twin spots of crimson appeared in her otherwise bloodless cheeks. I didn't know if she was going to pass out or explode.

I let the Darkness leak into my eyes, just a little. Enough to let her know I was a force to be reckoned with.

"Today, I learned that with a mere thought, I can control the whole of the Other World."

***

After Morgana left, I took a very long, very hot shower. Every inch of me felt grimy and grody. Climbing through the sewer system and rolling around in an enchanted forest would do that to you.

As I dried off, my tired brain tried to make sense of the whole Morgana situation. She was off my back for now, but I was pretty sure she hadn't entirely given up on whatever plan was floating around that psycho brain of hers. She wanted her people back in this world permanently and I doubted she would stop until she got what she wanted. On top of that, while we'd captured Darroch and gotten what intel we could from him, Alister was still on loose. Even worse? He had possession of the book, a book we still knew next to nothing about except it was apparently the key to, well, me.

My laptop chimed, indicating someone was trying to Skype me. I quickly threw on my robe and wrapped my hair in a towel before answering the call.

"Eddie!" I smiled as his face appeared on my screen. The connection was a little iffy, the picture and sound freezing and jumping around. "How are you? Aren't you on that steampunk cruise in the Caribbean?"

"Yes, in the Bahamas. Morgan, listen carefully. I..." The image froze for a second. "...danger. Discovered..." It froze again, this time for longer. I uselessly thumped the side of my screen as if it might help.

"Eddie? Are you there?"

"Need...help. Come quickly...dead."

"What? Eddie? Oh my gods, what's happening?"

There was a bit more jumping around of the screen, and then it zoomed in on one of Eddie's bespectacled eyes. "Hurry, Morgan. If you don't, we're all dead."

With that, the connection dropped entirely. No matter what I tried, I couldn't get him back.

I had to get to the Bahamas as fast as I could. I started running around the room, grabbing my things and throwing them randomly in my suitcase.

Airport. I needed to get to the airport. I could use the private plane. What island? I needed to find out where the ship was and fly to the nearest island. But what cruise line had Eddie taken?

Jack. I needed Jack.

I dashed out my door and down the hall to pound on his door. "Jack. Jack! Are you in there?" There was no answer. "Dammit."

I ran back to my room and grabbed my phone. I noticed I had a voicemail, but I didn't have time to listen. I needed to find out where Eddie was. Before I could dial, it rang. I frowned, not recognizing the number. I did recognize the country code, though. It was someone in the UK.

"Hello?"

"Morgan? This is Drago."

"Drago, hi. Listen..."

"I need you to come to Scotland as quickly as possible."

"I can't." I tossed a boot into my suitcase, then pulled it back out when I realized I'd need to wear it. "I have to catch a flight..."

"Yes, you do. To Edinburgh as fast as you can." I heard the urgency in his voice, and my blood ran cold.

"What's wrong, Drago?"

"It's Inigo."

The End

About Shea MacLeod

Shea MacLeod is the author of urban fantasy post-apocalyptic scifi paranormal romances with a twist of steampunk. She has dreamed of writing novels since before she could hold a crayon. She totally blames her mother

After a six year sojourn in London, England, a dearth of good donuts has driven her back to her hometown. She now resides in the leafy green hills outside Portland, Oregon where she indulges in her fondness for strong coffee, Ancient Aliens reruns, lemon curd, and dragons

Other Books by Shea MacLeod

<u>Sunwalker Saga</u>
Kissed by Darkness
Kissed by Fire
Kissed by Smoke

<u>Soulshifter:A Sunwalker Saga Spinoff</u>
Fearless

<u>Dragon Wars</u>
Dragon Warrior
Dragon Lord
Dragon Goddess

<u>Cupcake Goddess Novelettes</u>
Be Careful What You Wish For
Nothing Tastes As Good

Sign up to Shea MacLeod's Mailing List and be the first to hear about new releases:
http://sheamacleod.com/mailing-list-2

Please visit Shea MacLeod at
http://sheamacleod.wordpress.com

CPSIA information can be obtained
at www.ICGtesting.com
Printed in the USA
LVHW031541250219
608678LV00003B/514/P

9 780985 450649